"Where are we?"

"Why, you're in Wylder, ma'am. The prettiest little town in the whole Wyoming territory."

The smell of horse manure, dirty bodies, and dust swept up her nose. She wrinkled it as she gazed at the buildings around her. She saw lots of unpainted wood. No charming flower baskets sending cascades of blooms over porch railings.

Her gaze met the man's. "Are you sure this is Wylder?"

He nodded. "I am."

"This can't be. It isn't what I expected."

His gaze swept over the stagecoach and surrounding area before it rested on her again. "What exactly did you think you'd find here? Mansions and fancy carriages?"

He did not attempt to conceal his amusement.

"I didn't think it would be this dirty."

He smirked, then leaned close and lowered his voice. "It would seem to me that you'd feel right at home. After all, you came prepared, what with that ribbon of grime across that pretty face of yours."

She gasped. *How rude!*

Touching the brim of his hat with one hand, he turned and sauntered across the filthy street toward a big building. A sign dangled above the entrance steps, identifying the place as the Five Star Saloon.

It came as no shock that the first person she'd meet in Wylder was the town drunk. Her life had been out of control for months now. Why should it change because she'd traveled to the frontier?

Praise for Sarita Leone

"This was a great Christmas story. It keeps the reader interested all the way through to the end. I thoroughly enjoyed reading this book. If you love Christmas and romantic westerns, then you will definitely want to read this book."

~Sherrie Lea Morgan on *A Wylder Christmas*

~*~

"I thoroughly enjoyed reading *THE PIRATE'S PRIZE* by author Sarita Leone, and plan on reading more books by this talented author. From the beginning of the story, I was swept back in time and into the lives of these characters—and the story was never dull! The author's descriptions made it easy for me to visualize each character, and the story's ending was quite romantic. Looking forward to more books in The Lobster Cove Series—Five Stars!"

~Patti Jo Moore on *The Pirate's Prize*

Her Wylder Frontier

by

Sarita Leone

The Wylder West

Her Wylder Frontier

Cover Art by *Tina Lynn Stout*

The Wild Rose Press, Inc.
PO Box 708
Adams Basin, NY 14410-0708
Visit us at www.thewildrosepress.com

Publishing History
First Edition, 2022
Trade Paperback ISBN 978-1-5092-4015-9
Digital ISBN 978-1-5092-4016-6

The Wylder West Series
Published in the United States of America

Dedication

For my father, Macario Sepulveda.
I love you, Pop.
~*~
And for the husband who will always hold my heart.
Sempre per sempre, Vito.

Chapter 1

May 1879

"I don't care what the ticket says. This coach is taking us to Hell. And not straight there, either. This driver is taking the longest, dustiest, bumpiest route he can find." Lily Bloom blew a tendril of hair off her cheek. With breath as stale as one of the dirty canvas window coverings and eyelashes stiffened by trail dust, misery pervaded the cramped compartment. "I don't know how much longer I can do this. I'm not kidding, Daisy. I've reached the end of my ever-loving rope!"

Her companion on this journey westward didn't look up from her journal. Attention focused on the pen in her hand, she kept the same slow, steady pace she'd used through the entire trip. The implement crawled across the page. Every bump brought a scowl and the pages she'd written all looked like gibberish from Lily's vantage point, but the other's determination did not waver.

"What the hell is so all-fired interesting in that damn book of yours that you can't even look up at me when I'm speaking to you?" The rumbling of the huge wheels made it necessary to raise one's voice to be heard. Now, the level creeped higher, fueled by irritation and the longing for an ocean of hot water and a deep galvanized bathtub. "I know your ears work."

1

Lily knew patience did not come easily to her. It never had. Although she tried to be tolerant of her three sisters and their antics, it frustrated her that they needed so much attention. Like now, when the younger's focus should have been on her elder's comfort instead of that ink-spotted bundle of papers.

The sister who showed a challenging streak sat on the seat across from her. Beleaguering that they were siblings. Two personalities could not be more opposite than theirs, yet here they were, headed to Wyoming territory—better known as Hell. She felt certain it must be the case because, honestly, only the road to the underworld would be littered with the bones of the dead, the way this one must be. What else could the coach's wheels be bumping over, if not rotting carcasses and sun-bleached skeletons?

Daisy dotted a spot on the page with a flourish before she raised her gaze. She blew on the ink, closed the scuffed brown leather-bound book, and stuffed it with her pen into the carpet bag on the seat beside her. Rubbing her ink-stained fingertips together, she let out a long sigh.

"With all the cussing you're doing, I think you should expect to take a one-way trip to the devil's playground. Whatever would Father think if he could hear you now?" She flashed a sweet smile, but that didn't fool Lily. They were close enough in age that she knew the way the other's mind worked. Smiling like a debutante at a cotillion only hid the truth from those who didn't know the Bloom sister the way she did. Daisy had a spine of steel concealed behind bow-shaped lips and an endearing manner.

Their parents were safely back in Charleston with

their younger sister, Pansy. Reminding her that the head of the family wouldn't approve sank the conversation to a new depth.

"You seem to forget yourself. I'm the eldest, remember? Mother and Father are both proud of my accomplishments, and they fully endorse my acting my age. Your own lack of years shows when you say things like that. Take care. Your wild ways may be the death of you." She slipped her fingers into her hair, rooting around for the hairpin that had come loose enough for a lock to fall forward. A jab to put her hairdo back in place brought a sharp pain to her temple when she stabbed it with the pin. Not wanting to look gullible, she ignored the poke and fixed her hair. Then she sat back against the hard wooden seat and stared out the window.

The long trip westward wore on them both. The outset hadn't been particularly optimistic and as the miles stretched, they grew even less cheerful. Fleeing one's life did not bring pleasure, especially when the destination held so many unknowns.

She watched the endless stream of scrub, abandoned wagons, and occasional wooden cross marking a death on the trail outside the open window. It would be less dusty if she lowered the canvas, but the heat inside the coach reached unimaginable proportions when they tried that. She covered her nose with the less-than-fresh hanky she pulled from one sleeve and endured what could not be changed.

What could not be changed.

It never occurred to her she would leave their home city. Charleston, with its charm, fancy parties, and lifetime of memories held her heart. Not once had she imagined she wouldn't live all her days in the southern paradise.

But life has a way of surprising one. Fate did not care that she had her whole future planned when it threw an ugly tantrum, crashing her hopes against the cobblestone walk outside her door and leaving her heart shattered. She would not forget the cruel twist that brought her to this point. She did not doubt it would haunt her all her days.

A sideways glance across the interior of the coach showed Daisy living up to her name. Their snapping words did not affect her. Like her namesake, she bent in the breeze, unaffected by storms or unrest, content to grow in her own way at her own pace. The woman mystified Lily with her ability to shut out the world and find solace and contentment within her own mind and heart. There were times she admired her sister—and other times she came close to hating her—for this unique ability to accept life as it came to her and find joy regardless of the circumstances.

She did not have that in her.

She cleared her throat, hoping to get her sister's attention, but it went unnoticed. The other woman stared out as the miles passed. In true form, she probably formulated scenes for the stories she wrote and sent away for publication. She and the others who knew Daisy had learned that their words and actions— even those that should remain private—were fodder for the active imagination and might show up on a page.

Throat-clearing would not rouse her from her writer's mind, so she coughed into her hand. In true southern belle style, she made sure to be delicate about the gesture, yet intentionally did so as loudly as she ever had.

Her sister turned her gaze from the view. "Perhaps you should consider dropping the canvas on your side and sitting back. You don't want to arrive in Wylder with a consumptive disorder, do you?"

Lily did not fear the fatal illness. She did, however, sit back against the hard wood to prevent inhaling some trail dust. One could never be too careful where the lungs were concerned.

She brought her lips upward at their edges. A small smile, meant to calm the dissention between them. "Thank you for your concern. No, I do not wish to arrive in Wyoming territory in poor health. I am already so indisposed that adding to my constitutional distress would not be wise."

Watching her sister's face contort as she waged an internal battle between an unkind reply and keeping her own council would be amusing—if she herself did not sit squarely in the middle of the mental battlefield. There were so many instances in their lives when she'd witnessed Daisy trying to control her tongue that this did not come as a surprise.

The other's mouth dropped open. She stared for a long moment before it snapped shut. Favorable that she closed it right before the stage bounced over what must certainly be another cadaver skull. Had it still been gaping when they were jostled so high that the tops of their heads grazed the interior ceiling, she would have caught her tongue between her teeth.

She would have enjoyed seeing that.

"You cannot believe that you are experiencing any physical distress that is not related to this expedition. Your health is so sturdy that you put the rest of us to shame. Why, I recall how we all came down with the ague three winters ago—all of us, that is, except you. Dear sister, your constitution has never been subject to distress." The other woman glanced out the window. A smile played around the corners of her lips. When she turned back and met Lily's gaze, she added, "I do believe you are one of the strongest women I've ever met. Your body is fine. Your mind, however, may be in peril."

Dirty, tired, and out of sorts, it took a Herculean effort not to open the stage door and toss the other to the rutted road. She had it coming, not only for the remark about a perilous mind but for all the stony silences and displays of indifference she'd shown on this westward trek.

Instead of removing the offender from the coach, she took the high road. After all, it behooved her to do so, being the eldest and all.

"You seem to forget who nursed the lot of you through that miserable week. If I recall, your case included not only chills and fever, sister, but other less-agreeable complaints. Since I cleaned up after you, the least you can do is not be so perverse as to impugn my mind." She smiled pleasantly, hoping the message beneath the words found a spot to land.

All three of her sisters had presented a revolting mess that tested Lily's skill in the sickroom during the illness. Disgusting at the time, but now it served a purpose. A reminder for the other of her infirmity put her at a disadvantage. And she never minded putting any of her younger sisters in their places.

"I have not forgotten. How could I? You take every chance you can to bring up that miserable week. And unless I'm mistaken—which I am not—I've thanked you many times for caring for me." Her sister rummaged in a bag so large she could have hidden a small child in it. The notebooks and assorted writing implements she toted around weighed more than a toddler and made almost as much noise rattling together in the paisley bag. She pulled an ink-smudged handkerchief from its depths and held it out. "Here, you should wipe your face. You have an unfortunate slash of dirt across your skin, probably from leaning your head against the window frame."

She waved a hand in the air between them. "Get that filthy thing away from me. Really, how can you expect anyone to use that rag? It is covered with ink and who knows what else. No, thank you. I'm sure my face is fine."

A fast flick of the wrist sent the handkerchief back into the bag. Her sister snapped it shut as the stagecoach jolted to a stop. She sat forward and when the door opened, she exited the compartment. Looking back over her shoulder, she asked, "Well? Are you coming or are you going to Laramie?"

Laramie? Why, that sat fifteen miles past Wylder.

Lily grabbed her bag and went for the door. The steps were folded down, so she placed a foot on one and paused, half in and half out of the conveyance. The stagecoach stop looked bigger than many of the others. She wondered where on earth they were. The street bustled but this could not be their destination.

A tall man in dusty clothing stopped right beyond the steps. He stared at her for a long minute before he put out a hand to assist her.

"May I help you down, ma'am?" His faint northern

accent put her off, so she declined his assistance.

"I am perfectly capable of alighting from the carriage." She stepped down onto the hard-packed dirt. At the rear of the coach, Daisy directed two men in the removal of their bags. Lily turned to the stranger, who still stood regarding her with unconcealed interest. "Where are we?"

"Why, you're in Wylder, ma'am. The prettiest little town in the whole Wyoming territory."

The smell of horse manure, dirty bodies, and dust swept up her nose. She wrinkled it as she gazed at the buildings around her. She saw lots of unpainted wood. No charming flower baskets sending cascades of blooms over porch railings.

Her gaze met the man's. "Are you sure this is Wylder?"

He nodded. "I am."

"This can't be. It isn't what I expected."

His gaze swept over the stagecoach and surrounding area before it rested on her again. "What exactly did you think you'd find here? Mansions and fancy carriages?"

He did not attempt to conceal his amusement.

"I didn't think it would be this dirty."

He smirked, then leaned close and lowered his voice. "It would seem to me that you'd feel right at home. After all, you came prepared, what with that ribbon of grime across that pretty face of yours."

She gasped. *How rude!*

Touching the brim of his hat with one hand, he turned and sauntered across the filthy street toward a big building. A sign dangled above the entrance steps, identifying the place as the Five Star Saloon.

It came as no shock that the first person she'd meet in Wylder was the town drunk. Her life had been out of control for months now. Why should it change because she'd traveled to the frontier?

Chapter 2

The Five Star Saloon didn't serve as big a clientele during the daylight hours as it did most nights, but there were enough bodies in the place to make it feel welcome. That is, to a man used to frequenting saloons. At least that's what Theo surmised. The theory explained why he never felt at home in one. He availed himself of them so rarely that he didn't have a chance to grow accustomed to the smoke, smell, or sticky floors.

Back home in Philadelphia, his mother had run a strict household. No member of the family or staff would have ever stepped foot inside her home after imbibing. She would have fainted dead away if she knew he stood in a saloon now.

When Addison Merriweather walked through the batwing doors Theo breathed a sigh of relief. He had no idea why the man had requested this meeting, but now that he'd arrived they could get on with it. And then he'd be free to return to the homestead.

Although now that he thought of it, lingering in Wylder might prove interesting. That fiery vixen who'd stepped off the stage a few minutes ago caught his attention…

The beefy attorney walked over and held a hand out. They shook. Theo worked outdoors and had some muscle on him but exchanging greetings with the other man reminded him that a man could always build himself up some more.

"You have a nice, clean law office that would have done fine for this meeting." He tipped his hat back on his head when the other man stood beside him so he could meet his gaze without his eyes being in shadow. "Why are we here?"

When he'd last been in town, they'd run into each other in the mercantile. The attorney requested a meeting and, of course, he agreed. He knew the man to be an upstanding citizen—he was a lawyer, for Pete's sake—and he had a firm belief that if they were to tame the west at all, good men should band together.

They'd set the time and place. Now that they were side by side, he couldn't help but wonder what the other man had on his mind. Fortunately, he didn't have to wait long to find out.

The bartender came over, swiping at the bar with a grimy rag.

Addison held up two fingers and said, "Whiskey. And try to find clean glasses."

A grin from the man on the other side, who reached beneath the bar and came up with two sparkling shot glasses. He set them down, filled them, and nodded his thanks as he slid the lawyer's money off the bar and into his pocket.

The other held up his glass and smiled. "When two men discuss business, it's wise to raise a glass to what we hope will be a mutually beneficial arrangement." He downed the whiskey, so Theo did the same. "Listen, I heard that you've got a cavern on your property. Sometimes those spots are rich with iron ore. I know your brother Thomas is a mining investor. I am, too. I figure that maybe if the three of us put our heads together, we might pull some money outta that cave. What do you think?"

He and Thomas had already discussed mining the cave. They'd even considered asking Addison to join in on their venture. But they didn't figure to work the mine until a couple of years passed. Too much to do now getting the homestead property running at full potential to fritter away time in the cave.

"Well, we'd be agreeable to that." He waved the offer of a second whiskey away. His head already felt muddled, and he'd only had the one shot. "But we don't plan to work the mine for a while. A couple of years, maybe."

Addison nodded. "That's what I hoped, actually. I'm tied up with more legal work than I can handle right now." He looked around at the men gathered behind them. Tables held card players. Others were filled with ranch hands anxious to spend their pay. Still more sat alone, staring into their libations as if searching for answers to questions only they heard. "Wylder has its share of lawlessness. I think me an' the sheriff will be busy for a good while." He turned his gaze on Theo and shrugged. "I'm just thinkin' long term, is all."

There were few men he'd consider teaming up with, aside from Thomas. Addison was one on his short list of partners, so he nodded.

"Then long term, we've got an understanding." Theo shook the man's hand a second time, and again he felt the power of the other. He didn't doubt that the attorney could subdue a man in a barroom brawl as effortlessly as he proved his points in the judge's chamber. "First, though, I have to get the homestead settled more to my liking, you realize."

"I get what you're saying." He held up a hand to the bartender. When Theo waved the second offer away again, he dropped one finger and ordered a single whiskey for himself. "You don't have a wife, do you?"

Theo gave a disgusted snort, the kind his old mother would look disdainfully upon. But the booze had loosened his inhibitions a bit. "Nope—but not for lack of looking. There aren't a whole lot of available women…not unless you're of a mind to take a widow with children or a soiled dove trying to turn respectable. And while I don't judge a man who fancies that type, I'm not one of them."

Beside him, the man set his elbows on the bar. He lifted his glass and swirled the amber liquid inside. "I get your meaning bein' as I'm in the same predicament. Wouldn't do for a man in my position to take up with a woman with a shady past. Not many to choose from who don't bring some baggage with them, though."

The man's words rang true. Theo thought he'd looked over every unattached female in Wylder, considered her wife potential, and discarded each. Sure, some were fine women who would make another man happy, but he didn't see one who ignited even a glimmer of a spark within him.

And he needed spark.

"They all have baggage. Every single one of them show up in town totin'—"

It hit him that he'd just met a woman. With actual baggage. And sass that brought a spark to the center of his chest.

Addison nudged him with a shoulder. "What put

that smile on your face?"

He shook his head. "Nothing. Not really."

The other man downed his shot, then slammed the empty on the bar upside down. "You do realize I'm a lawyer and I separate the truth from the bull on a daily basis, right? That shit-eating grin on your face comes from something. Spill it."

He turned and locked gazes with the man beside him. "Do you believe in fate? What I mean to say is, do you think a man can be walking down the street mindin' his own business when something falls right in his path that will change his whole life?"

The attorney's eyebrows rose as he considered the question. "I've seen crazier things than that in my time dealing with the law, so I've gotta say I think it's possible. Not probable, mind you, but sure, it could happen. Why? Do you think fate's dropped something special onto your lap?"

A jolt shot up his spine. On his lap? Damn, he'd like to get that beautiful but snippy woman on his lap! He'd wipe the grime off that pretty face and hug her until the jagged edges wore away.

"Honestly, I think so."

A slap of the other's beefy hand against the bar. "Well, then, that calls for a celebratory shot. No, don't try to decline. When Lady Luck comes callin' we need to give thanks." He leaned across the bar and called to the bartender. "Two more over here—we've got a woman to toast!"

At that, a cheer went up from the room. Theo smiled, nodded to those who lifted their drinks in salute, and shook his head. Father told him that when he met the woman he'd want for a wife, he'd know. And after the prickly exchange beside the stagecoach, he felt pretty sure he'd met her.

Now to convince her that they should form an association. Hard to do when he didn't even know her name.

Chapter 3

Lily tapped a toe on the dirt. She would have crossed her arms, but to do so she'd have to put her bag on the ground—and that did not appeal. No need to add more filth to her favorite traveling bag.

Daisy's arms were wrapped around their sister. Her bag sat at their feet. Typical behavior, to let things fall where they may without worry for consequences—or what mess anything might land in.

The sisters hugged as if they hadn't seen each other in decades. It made no sense; Violet had only been gone from home a little more than a year. This unseemly display showed ill behavior.

As the eldest, it fell to her to remind the others of their manners.

She cleared her throat. When no one responded, she cleared it a second time with such force that it pained her.

The man standing at Violet's elbow turned her way. She guessed him to be the luggage handler, although a bit long in the tooth for the job and too well-dressed. The faint lines at the corners of his eyes and single sliver of white near his temple led her to believe he must be in his late thirties. Too old for a porter in Charleston but apparently not for the frontier.

She snapped her fingers and pointed to the bags. "These are ours. And this one, as well." She held her bag out toward the man. When he didn't immediately take it from her, she gave her wrist a shake. "The one by my sister's feet, also—although I do hope she hasn't dropped it in something disagreeable. Lord knows, we can do without adding a stink to a welcome that's already putrid."

He touched the brim of his hat with one hand, took her bag from her with the other, then bent down and picked up Daisy's. He put them in the back of a nearby wagon. Their two trunks followed the bags.

Her sisters broke apart, finally. Violet turned and reached for her, but Lily took a step back.

"I am covered with grit. You don't want to get mussed, although I imagine our dear sister has already transferred her grime to your pretty outfit." Violet's periwinkle blue skirt, matching hat and jacket, made her look like she'd tumbled from a bird's nest. Bright against the dreary street, she brought cheer to the gloomy scene.

"I don't care about any of that. It is so good to see you—I must have a hug!" She stepped forward and pulled her into an embrace. Speaking softly against her cheek, she said, "I've missed you."

Excess sentiment did not get anyone anywhere in life, so she did not generally partake of sloppy emotions. Her last foray into honesty with another led her to…well, it dumped her off on this dirty street, is what it had done. No, no more emotional exchanges for her.

Pulling away, she murmured, "Yes, well that is nice."

She didn't miss the look that passed between her sisters. They had no way of knowing how it felt to walk in her shoes, so they should keep their smug expressions to themselves.

Time to remind them about who led the family.

"Let's not squander time standing about in the street like a trio of ragamuffins. I have already directed the porter to load our baggage. I suggest we make our way to your home now, Violet." She pulled her reticule higher on her wrist and clasped her arms across her chest. It wouldn't do to be robbed so quickly upon her arrival. "I hope it's not too dreadfully far from here. I need a long, hot bath and some sustenance. We have been on the trail so many days that I feel wrung out."

Her sister shot her a questioning look. "Where did you find a porter in Wylder?"

She heard Daisy snicker but that, too, she chose to ignore. With a nod toward the man who stood at the back of the other two, she said, "Why, right there, behind you. And as he's placed our baggage in that wagon, I assume that is our transport. So can we get going?"

Her sister's lips drew into a thin line as her brows lowered. Her gaze grew hard. She reached a hand out and drew the man forward. She took a step to the right and brought him into the circle of sisters, so close that Lily got a whiff of tobacco and wood smoke. She wasn't a fan of tobacco use but it beat the scent of animal droppings pervading the air in front of the stagecoach office.

"This is Mister Harvey. He is not a baggage man. Thomas is the man I am keeping company with since last Christmas." She narrowed her eyes. "I would be offended, but I will forgive your lapse in judgment. I am sure Thomas will, as well, as it is clear you are discombobulated from your journey and are not making sense."

In other circumstances, she would have turned on her heel and stormed off. The audacity of a younger sister speaking to her in such a haughty tone could not be tolerated. But since she had no idea where she would flounce off to, and nothing in Heaven could convince her to return to Charleston in that bumpy chariot traveling over Satan's highway, she remained. Staring into her sister's eyes, she saw the truth of things.

This sister had changed since leaving Charleston. No longer the mousy schoolteacher looking for her place in the world, she'd turned into someone almost unrecognizable. The younger woman had arrived, found her footing, and lost her heart. That last showed so clearly in the strong gaze that gripped hers that shock sped through her.

So wrong for her sister to find love when she had recently lost it. The firstborn led, the younger siblings followed. How could they flaunt the rules of society this way?

Swallowing around the ice on her tongue, she met the man's gaze and tipped her chin. "Mister Harvey."

Chapter 4

The wagon stopped in front of a house surrounded by a white picket fence. Built on a side lane and insulated from the clamor and intensity of the main streets. Amazing what a little distance could do. A bell chimed but it did not sound close, although she imagined it could not be too far away.

Lily swept her gaze over the small dwelling. It did not look anything like the home in Charleston where they were raised. There were no wrought-iron gates, gingerbread swirls at the eaves, or wrap-around porches. No hanging baskets dripped with scarlet geraniums or concrete basins filled with splashing birds.

Violet's house did not lack charm, though. The fence looked new, and a wide porch ran the width of the building. Buckets filled with flowers she did not recognize sat beside the gray gravel walkway.

Unlike so many structures they'd passed traveling through town, paint covered the wooden clapboards on this one. She guessed her sister had mixed the shade herself, because surely no self-respecting mercantile would stock this color.

Pale violet siding, with white window and door trim, and a dark purple front door made the house stand out from the others on the street. She wanted to chide her sibling for such an irresponsible choice but could not because, in her heart, she loved the way the little house looked.

It is like Violet.

Brilliance and beauty, in balance and on display without fear—that her sister came to life in wood, glass, and hardware sent a sharp twinge of jealousy up her spine. Leave it to Violet to find her place in the world long before she did. It did not seem fair—and she did not like it.

The others grabbed the luggage while she waited beside the wagon. They chattered, laughed, and seemed delighted to be in each other's company, while she stood like a neglected, forgotten statue in some overgrown park. It would not do.

She turned to them. "Must we remain out here in this insufferable heat all day? Violet, I have traveled many miles to be here with you. The least you can do is offer me a place to freshen up and take my rest. Instead, you leave me rotting in the sun."

The man who kept company with her sister shot her a look. Fortunately for him, he kept his lips buttoned. Looks she could ignore. Comments she would not abide. Whatever his position in her sister's life, he had best see from the outset that he had no say in hers.

Violet had her bag in one hand, but she did not offer to relieve her of the burden. Filled with books, it had weight to it. She'd toted it across Hell's wasteland. Now someone else could shoulder the burden.

"Don't be rude. We have only arrived, and you'll have sister sending us back home on the next stagecoach if you don't mind your mouth." Daisy came up and stood beside her, a scowl on her face. She carried her carpetbag as if it were empty. "What would Mother say if she could hear you speak this way?"

Typical for her, to not complain but act as if everything were a grand adventure. The next story for her dreadful publishing habit probably already born in the overactive imagination.

"Mother is not here and as the eldest Bloom west of the Mississippi, it falls to me to take the role of matriarch in our mother's stead. So mind your own manners, and see that you treat me with the respect that is my due." A sharp nod to the scowling sister before she turned to their hostess. "Violet? Are you going to show us in, or shall I take a room at the hotel?"

Mister Harvey deposited the trunks on the porch while they were speaking. Now, he opened the door with a flourish, bowed, and said, "Allow me, ladies."

Violet laughed at his outlandish behavior, as did Daisy. She, however, did not appreciate theatrics on a good day—and this wasn't a good day. Tired, dirty, and out of sorts, she swept up the walkway, onto the porch, and past the impudent man.

Her sisters followed, giggling like magpies.

She stopped short when she saw who waited in the front hallway. A smiling Chinese woman, wearing house slippers—which meant she belonged in the place. The woman nodded and opened her mouth to speak, but Lily cut her off.

She turned to her sister. "How on earth can you afford servants on a teacher's wages?"

Chapter 5

Had she not been so disgruntled she would have laughed at the expression on Violet's face. Her sister had changed, but some things were not affected—like her temper, which she still had not learned to hide.

Her sibling's violet eyes rounded, color rose in her cheeks, and she opened—then closed—her mouth twice before speaking between gritted teeth. "You cannot come into my home and insult Lin. She is like a sister to me, and you are not allowed to treat her badly." The words were clipped but grew louder until she came close to shouting. "Do you hear me?"

She took a step back. The temper did not shock her, but the intensity of this storm reached a level never before seen from the mild Violet.

"Don't be silly. Everyone can hear you. The drunk out by the saloon can hear you—so keep your voice down, sister. It is unwise and wholly disrespectful to speak to me this way."

A tendril hung beside their hostess' face, escaped from her otherwise-tidy hairdo. The fail disappointed Lily. Her lessons in securing hair pins had flopped with this sister, as the wisp showed.

Her sister pushed her hair back from her face and stared into her eyes. A vein throbbed in her temple.

The others had fallen away. In Lily's mind, the room held the two of them, and it felt as if they were in a sparring match that would allow for only one victor to leave the ring. As the oldest, she must reign victorious. Her sister must realize that.

Offering olive branches did not come naturally but in the interest of putting this hellacious day behind her, and perhaps getting fed something other than dusty trail food, she forced a smile. Reaching out a hand, she tucked the wayward hair behind her sister's ear, the way she had when they were younger.

"I did not mean to disrespect you or your...ahem, your friend, although I do not see how you would need any more 'sisters' in your life. Good heavens, there are four of us. That is more than enough sisterhood for anyone." She turned to the Chinese woman who had stepped to the side and flattened herself against the wall. The beautiful dark eyes held no malice. "I regret my hasty assumption. It will not happen again, I assure you."

And it would not, because she had no intention of addressing this person in the future. Violet could feel however she wanted about her, for now. But that would change. She would see to it.

Their parents would have spasms if they knew what sort of existence their daughter lived. Chinese interlopers standing in for family members, baggage porters for courting purposes, and purple houses, of all things! This would not do.

The other woman did not reply, but she did give a quick chin dip. Sufficient enough to move the conversation along.

She pulled her lips into a smile and met Violet's gaze. The apology that did not claim responsibility or display heartfelt remorse did not fool her sister. It showed in her eyes that she saw beyond the lie. She, too, must have peace uppermost in her mind because she nodded.

"Don't do it again. I won't have anyone disrespected in my home. Do you understand me?" No stretch to imagine the other's classroom. The schoolteacher voice she used now cautioned that if one did not adhere to her rules, there would be erasers to clean later.

"Really, you needn't be so harsh. Why, if you would prefer I not stay with you, I'm sure I can get this gentleman friend of yours to take me to the nearest hotel." She pointed to her bags. "It's not as if I've crossed the wilderness with the barest necessities to be mistreated by my own family. If your friend does not wish to help me, I'm sure I can drag my trunk down the street—point me in the proper direction." Her gloves were in her hand, so she tugged the left on. It had a dark spot near one fingertip. Lord knows what that could be but there must be a mercantile in this godforsaken place. She'd purchase a new pair in short order.

Daisy and the man stood back and watched without speaking. Between them and the Chinese woman, they were surrounded by gaping sculptures. A horrid welcome to a nasty town, then.

She knew her sister most likely sided with Violet. It had been that way since they were children, so she expected it. And the man was her sister's acquaintance, so she assumed he backed her, too.

Fine. No stranger to being the odd one out, she shoved her fingers into the remaining glove and took a step toward the door.

Daisy put out a hand to stop her. "As usual, you are

being ridiculous. You're hungry, and you know how unreasonable you can be when you need to be fed. So why not thank our sister for welcoming us into her home? And then, perhaps, you should consider not speaking for a while."

There comes a moment when one is too overwrought to fight, even when one is in the right. Weariness washed over her.

Daisy's green eyes were the color of forest ferns, a soft shade that women envied, and men could not resist. They were one of the woman's greatest physical attributes. A hint of steel showed in them now, turning the color closer to gray than green.

Heaving a sigh, she turned to their hostess. The color had drained from her sister's cheeks and the vein throbbed less stridently in her temple. Anger had not left her gaze entirely, but it had lessened.

"Thank you for your hospitality, Violet. It is kind of you to welcome us into your home."

Chapter 6

Theo gave his house a long look with a critical eye. He tipped his head to one side, then the other. Then, he brought his gaze horizontal and stood for several moments taking in the sight of it. He loved the place and saw only straight lines and sturdy shelter from the outside world. The building protected from the elements and would also serve as a safe place in the event hostiles of any sort breached his fences.

He recognized security in the homestead, but what would a woman see? He'd had little to do with them but knew well enough that women and men did not think alike.

Thomas built the place for his wife, daughter, and the child they hoped to see born within its walls. That plan did not come to fruition, and his brother sold the homestead to him after the unfortunate event that left him a widower charged with raising Alexia on his own.

Two graves beneath a spreading cottonwood tree, a reminder that life on the western frontier had its harsh moments, were well tended. Thomas visited often, leaving flowers for the those he'd buried.

Hopefully, another woman would find the homestead appealing, despite the sadness that made him its owner.

His brother interrupted his musing by walking up behind him and clapping a hand on his shoulder. "You look lost in thought, Theo. What's rattling through that head of yours?"

They walked toward the front porch. Up a couple of steps, to the chairs lined up near the railing, where they settled.

"Merriweather and I had a meeting about mining the cave out here. Not now, but sometime down the line." He turned to face Thomas and saw he didn't look surprised. "You already knew about his interest?"

"I did. After all, we do work within spitting distance of each other."

"What do you think about it?"

"Told him he'd have to talk with you. This is your place, not mine." He sucked in a deep breath, then let it out slowly. "But I think it's sound thinking. That cave could hold a whole lotta something—or a whole lotta nothing—but there's no way of knowing unless you look."

Thomas had a head for business. If he stood behind the idea, it must be solid.

"Exactly what I'm thinking. So in a couple of years we'll see what's in there. In the meantime, I intend to work the land." He spread his arms wide. "Look at this place. It's gorgeous."

The other swept his gaze over the spread laid out before them. A tidy fence surrounded the house. Outbuildings to provide shelter for livestock. A garden patch. The lane leading into the distance which connected the self-sufficient spread with what lay beyond. And, toward the horizon, craggy mountains.

"I think so. But then, I'm the one who chose it." Thomas turned to him and shrugged. "I suppose it's good you like it, too. After all, you ended up with the place."

Sadness draped Thomas' shoulders like a low-hanging cloud. It always did after he visited the gravesite but, thankfully, didn't linger. Theo didn't know how a man put aside such anguish, but his brother managed to do it.

He kept his tone even. "I'm sorry for what led to my buying you out, but I'm grateful to be keeper of this bit of God's green earth." He paused, torn between bringing up what weighed on his mind or saving it for another time. But unless he went to town to talk with his brother, the circumstances would be the same next time they saw each other. Thomas would arrive with flowers, go to his family's burial site, then return to sit a spell on the porch. Might as well speak now. "Thomas, I'm thinking it's time I had a wife."

His brother turned to him with a hopeful smile. "I agree. You need a good woman."

He didn't point out that the mourning period had long past and Thomas hadn't taken that nice Violet Bloom to the church yet. Maybe things were different for widowers.

"That's what I'm thinking. This place needs a woman's touch. And…" He hesitated.

"What is it, Theo?"

He shrugged. "And I'm lonely, is all."

Thomas reached across the distance between their chairs and slapped a hand on his shoulder. "Of course you are. Men and women need each other. Not only for the marital bed—which, believe me, keeps a man going from day to day—but for companionship. This place must be awful quiet for one person. I think it's great you're thinking of a wife. Got anyone particular in mind?"

Theo scraped a hand across his cheek. He knew he wouldn't see anyone save his brother, so he hadn't shaved. His whiskers whispered against his palm as he considered his reply.

"Well, it's like this…Yesterday two women got off the stage. One with pretty green eyes and the other…well, let's just say the second one had more mouth than the first—and she wasn't afraid to use it." He stopped and scraped the other cheek. "Can't say I ever thought myself the type to be attracted to an outspoken woman, but it seems I might be. That one, she lit a spark in me that I can't seem to shut down."

His brother threw his head back and laughed. No explanation, just a loud laugh that sounded pulled from his feet. Theo smiled, grateful that the post-cemetery visit cloud had disappeared.

"What the hell's so funny?" He pretended outrage—but kept the smile on his face.

As he wiped his eyes, Thomas shook his head. "Those women? They're Violet's sisters—two more Bloom beauties from back east." He sucked in a deep breath and met Theo's gaze. His eyes glistened, tears from laughing so hard that were preferable to the grieving ones he'd worn so often in the past. "The green-eyed sister is Daisy. And the one with the viper tongue? She's the eldest, Lily." He snapped his fingers and pointed to Theo's chest. "Wait a minute! You didn't see me standing near the stagecoach with Violet yesterday?"

A fast head shake. "Nope. All I saw were two women. One caught my attention real quick—and it wasn't because she had that traveling grime across her face." He brought her face to his mind and smiled. Lily. The name suited her. "The minute I saw her step off that coach, put her foot on Wylder soil, and wrinkle that pretty little nose, I thought 'Now that's a woman.'"

Thomas nodded, a grin playing around his lips as he fought to keep a straight face. "Well, you got that much right. She's a woman—and I reckon' she'll keep you occupied so well that you won't feel a bit lonely."

Chapter 7

Sleep was an elusive bedfellow, despite the fatigue that sat heavy on Lily's heart.

Nightmares, a constant companion in her nocturnal hours since Warren's accident, had not been left behind. They traveled along, finding her even as she put miles between herself and South Carolina.

The past did not respect the present, intruding even when one begged it not to do so.

None of the rooms in the house were large, including the bedrooms. With space for two beds, a washstand, two small side tables, and a trunk at the foot of the other bed, it accommodated them, but only. Lacking space to store their clothing, they left off proper unpacking, so travel luggage occupied all remaining floor space.

Daisy's soft breathing came from across the room. Moonlight from the window showed she slept on her back, with her arms flung wide on the pillow, as if she were a babe without a care in the world. Envious of the unencumbered nature of the sister's slumber, she turned her back on her.

How dare she sleep so easily when her sibling suffered so greatly? It defied rational thinking—but then, she had been born into a thoughtless sisterhood. If they were bananas, she would be the only unblemished fruit in the bunch.

When the door opened with a tiny squeak, her heart faltered. Slow footsteps crossed over the threshold and into the room.

Her mind raced, searching for possible explanations. Clearly, they were about to be murdered in their sleep! She had heard of such goings-on. The west hadn't earned the nickname "Wild West" without reason, but she hadn't thought that she would become a victim in such short order. Why, Violet lived out here for more than a year and no one had slit her throat yet.

Her own bad luck that her first night in Wylder would also be her only night.

She heard gentle padding, so soft as to be nearly silent. She surmised the interloper must be from one of the Native tribes that were so unruly in the territory. News of their mayhem made headlines back home, although the stories were often tucked discreetly into the furthest pages of the Charleston Daily News. It would not do to place the disturbing news too close to the front where women with delicate constitutions might see it. But they trekked through the forests and were known for their stealth so it made sense that they would arrive on silent feet.

Either that, or the Chinese woman had come to kill her.

Well, she did not travel through Hell to die in an uncanopied, plain pine bedstead.

Her fingers tightened around the lumpy pillow beneath her head. Not feather down, like at home. This rock-hard chunk encased in muslin made a decent weapon. She would have preferred the Remington under-over derringer Father had gifted her, but it rested on the bedside table.

From now on she planned to sleep with the gun beneath her pillow. That is, if she lived to see tomorrow.

The intruder drew near and placed something on the bed. It dipped at the footboard, so she did not stir. To scalp her or slit her throat, the killer would need to get closer.

She sensed movement near her shoulders.

Her heart froze and her mind went blank. If she had any chance to save her life, she must act.

With every ounce of energy in her body, she sat up, swung the pillow in an arc, and screamed. "Not tonight! You won't kill me tonight, damn you!"

The pillow knocked the assailant to the floor. She threw it down and reached for the gun. In the darkness, she knocked the weapon to the floor. The clunk of steel hitting pine boards made her heart skip a beat.

Damn it!

"What are you doing?" The pillow came flying back up to the bed but missed hitting her. She hung halfway off the mattress, her fingers searching for the missing derringer. "Lily Mae Bloom—what is wrong with you, attacking me like that? I nearly broke my neck!"

That voice.

"Violet?" She found the gun and wrapped her fingers around it. "Is that you?"

"Of course it's me! Who did you expect would come in to bring extra blankets for you and Daisy?"

Daisy struck a match and lit the bedside lamp. Holding it aloft, she surveyed the scene.

Their hostess sprawled on the floor, a blanket in a puddle beside her. Lin stood in the doorway, clad in an intricately embroidered nightdress. Lily lay half in and half out of her bed, with a gun clutched in one hand.

"What in tarnation are you two doing? Can't you confine your romps to daylight hours?" A smug smile played around the corners of Daisy's lips. She loved seeing her eldest sister indisposed and made no secret of the fact.

Lily had pulled something in her side when she swung the pillow. A stitch brought a gasp of pain as she tried to pull herself back into the bed.

Violet noticed instantly, turning her tone from outraged to compassionate. "What's wrong? Did you hurt yourself?"

She screwed up her eyes and fought a wave of discomfort. Whatever lay beneath the skin above her right hip did not appreciate the wild defensive movements she had made. It spasmed, sending a spear of pain across her lower back.

She waved Violet away when her sister tried to help her.

Better to get up under her own steam and show them both that no matter what happened, she remained in full control. Fighting a fresh wave of agony, she squeezed her eyes closed and hauled herself back into the bed.

It required all her strength to move. Apparently, when she summoned that power, it affected her fingers as well as her other bodily muscles. At the exact moment her sister's friend stepped into the room, Lily managed to sit upright in the bed.

At the same instant the tiny gun discharged, sending a blinding flash and a deafening pop into the confined space.

Chapter 8

If she were home in Charleston, Lily would be busy resting up for the evening's festivities. That's what every well-bred unattached young woman did on Saturday, prepare herself to be the most charming, beautiful, captivating woman she could possibly be.

And everyone knew magic like that, week after week until a marriage proposal was secured, took effort. Lots of it.

She wished she were home now, working on becoming sublimely irresistible. Lounging about with cold compresses on her eyes to minimize swelling and make the whites so bright they looked like stars plucked from the night sky. Using sugar water and muslin to tear off wayward eyebrow hairs. Enduring paraffin gloves despite their heat because a woman should be willing to tolerate discomfort to be stunning—and soft hands stroked a man's ego, even when cloaked in white gloves.

She'd done all that, had been the belle of the ball, and made a solid, profitable match.

Despite many old families finding themselves in reduced circumstances after the war, Warren Fielding's proved an exception. They maintained their fortune, or most of it, anyhow. Some said they sold their currency for gold coins they stashed for the duration of the war, but no one knew—and she didn't care. So long as the

Fielding family maintained their social standing, joining the Bloom family to theirs offered advantages to both sides.

Planning a wedding, that's what she should be considering. She'd found a suitable man, accepted his proposal, and intended to marry him. She hoped to eventually learn to love him, but if that didn't happen she would accept that fate as part of the price she paid to be settled—and, most importantly, held in high social regard.

But Warren's carelessness changed everything. Her future security, gone in an instant. One ill-fated jump over a fallen tree log on his favorite horse, an "unfortunate" injury, and it all came to a screeching halt.

She would have gone on with the nuptials, but he wouldn't hear of it. No, his stubborn refusal to carry on despite the regrettable event upended her entire life. The man had no regard for anyone save himself. Had he been a woman, he would've married her. Women knew there are more important considerations than what happens behind closed bedchamber doors.

And it wasn't as if the man had been particularly well-endowed or skillful in that area. It had been her first and only experience, that one time he stepped over the line and drew her into the shadows beyond the terrace at the Applegate estate. Enough, that frantic fumbling, messy, wet kisses, scotch-infused breath on her neck and awkward crush against a moss-covered pillar, to convince her that part of married life would not be the best. The compact nature, both of the act itself and her partner's anatomy, gave her cause to question whether it had occurred. Only a smear of pink and unpleasant stickiness on her thigh convinced her that what he had done did in fact count as the one act she'd been warned against.

It seemed hardly worth the effort to save oneself for something so trivial.

Following the Applegate mess, as she thought of it, Warren had become almost docile, as affectionate and accommodating as a lap cat. The gifts he lavished afterward were extravagant. She wondered if he would do the same after they were married. Garnet bracelets and emerald stick pins, payment for his pleasure. If so, she would gladly fill her jewelry chest with post-coital trinkets.

Then the riding accident and his obstinate cancellation of their match swept away everything.

And landed her here, in the middle of the wilderness without any hope of a genteel future.

No lounging about in Wylder on Saturday mornings, either. Violet and Daisy, as well as that Chinese woman who lived in the small house, waited for her downstairs. They were going to town, whatever that meant.

She looked over her dresses, wondering what one wore to walk along grimy streets, stepping over drunks and dodging bullets. Hopefully, this outing wouldn't take them back to the area near the saloon. She'd seen enough of that gritty spot already. Besides, that man might be hanging around still. He probably lived in the saloon.

"Lily? What's taking so long?" Violet's voice held a schoolteacher's unspoken challenge that whatever kept her sister had best be something she deemed important. "Get a wiggle on, please. We don't want to lose the morning waiting for you."

It sat on the tip of her tongue to holler down that they should go ahead without her. She didn't want to see any more of this place, anyhow. But being cooped up in this tiny, hot room did not excite her, either.

She looked down at herself. The dark blue bodice had long sleeves to protect her arms from the sun as well as secure her modesty. The skirt, patterned with a smaller bustle than last year's fashions, gathered in flattering waves across her hips and thighs.

It would have to do because she didn't fancy changing her costume.

Footsteps alerted her to the second wave of sisterly impatience. Daisy had yet to learn to convey herself with less enthusiasm than a lady should, despite all her admonitions. Oh, well, there were less likely to be distractions in the Wyoming territory so she might be able to get her younger sister in hand. A silver lining to the current mess, she supposed.

The bedroom door opened and, as she'd suspected, Daisy appeared. Her brow furrowed when she met Lily's gaze.

"Whatever is taking you so long? Honestly, Lily. You know we're waiting for you, yet you act as if you're the only one affected by your dawdling." She put a hand on her hip and tapped a toe against the floorboard.

Without bothering to respond to the childish outburst, she pinned her bonnet in place. Yesterday's dishevelment had been a one-time display. These Wylder people would not see tendrils waving about her temples or smudges of trail grime on her cheek again.

When she felt satisfied with her image in the

looking glass, she turned and gave her sister a once-over. Her beauty could not be denied, or even diminished by the ink-stained fingers gripping her hip.

Still, she must point out any area to be improved upon. Lord knew, her sister would have a time finding a man to put up with her bookish ways and incessant scribbling. The chore of providing direction to the younger Bloom fell squarely on her shoulders.

"Perhaps you might consider taking extra care with your appearance." She waved a hand toward the other's fingers. "This is the wild west but that doesn't mean you should leave off basic grooming. Really, those hands are worse than a field hand's—how do you expect to catch a husband with fingers that look as if you dip them in coal dust?"

"I don't plan to 'catch' anything or anyone, and that includes a man, so concern yourself with other topics." She turned and headed out the door but paused to add, "It seems you're the one who is in the market for a suitor. You know, to replace the one you had in Charleston."

Chapter 9

Walking down Wylder Street bore no resemblance to strolling along Charleston's shaded stone lanes, where one could taste history on the breeze wafting in from the harbor and fall under the spell of the clip-clopping of horse-drawn carriages.

Lily wrinkled her nose as a mule, led by a filthy man wearing rags, passed. That he tilted his head and flashed a toothless grin did nothing to diminish her revulsion.

She blamed Warren for this. Him and his stupid horse and their even more ridiculous riding accident. Were it not for them, she would be at dress fittings with Mother. Instead, she traipsed along a dusty street with a sister who seemed intent on making her more miserable. As if that were even possible.

"I see the expression on your face. You hate it here already, and you haven't even given Wylder a chance." Violet placed a hand on her arm and gave a gentle squeeze before she removed it. "Don't be so quick to judge. There are lots of good people here. Before you know it, you'll fit right in."

Her sister smiled and tipped her head to several people they passed. It seemed she knew everyone in this godforsaken place.

"Fit in? Good heavens! If I ever look like that's happening, take your pistol from your pocket and shoot me, sister. Please, put me right out of my misery." She avoided meeting anyone's gaze and on the one or two occasions that someone caught her eye and nodded, she pretended she hadn't seen them. "I don't know how on earth you abide this place."

Buildings lined the street. So far she'd spotted a jail and sheriff's office, further proof that they walked mean streets surrounded by nefarious characters. A law office and bank sat within shooting distance of each other. She imagined lawyers could chat with criminals as they rushed from the bank. Definitely a convenient set up—if one didn't get shot trying to pick up business.

Her sister smiled at a child who passed before turning and giving her a scowl, equal in intensity to the smile but without any of the charm. "How can you even say that? You're being your usual ornery self. That obviously didn't work out for you back home and it's not going to here, either."

How dare she speak of home so blithely?

"You have no idea what you're talking about." She held her handkerchief to her nose as they passed a trio of mules tied to a hitching post. The animals were heavily laden with mining supplies. "Living in this frontier has made you forget yourself and what home looks like. Why, I doubt you'd recognize a lawn party if one fell at your feet."

Daisy and that dreadful Chinese woman had left to go heaven knew where and do heaven knew what. She should have put a stop to the plan when it arose, but she'd had enough of watching over the impetuous author among them. Let her find out how it felt to be in this place on her own. Hopefully she wouldn't get into any predicament that would require her assistance. She didn't feel well and did not have the disposition to put up with shenanigans.

She supposed the others thought she and Violet would have a heart-to-heart talk as they sauntered through town. Clearly, they did not recognize the unlikelihood of that.

"Lily, I tried to be open about this situation but you're not making it easy. Honestly, you're trying my patience and I fear I may say something regrettable."

They'd reached a large building with a wide wooden walkway that ran the length of it. Up three steps from the street, it offered some respite from the horse, mule, and foot traffic.

She looked at the sign hanging above the door. Wylder's Mercantile.

They stopped at the edge of the walkway, out of the way and in a fairly private spot.

Her stomach still hadn't settled from being tossed about by the stagecoach. It roiled now, sending a clamminess to her neck and forehead that did nothing to improve her mood.

"Whatever is on your mind, feel free to say it." She wiped her handkerchief across her forehead, then blotted her neck with a shaky hand. "You know how much I value honesty. And Mother, she would not like us holding harsh words unsaid between us. So if you feel you have something to say, get it over with so we may move on."

Her sister tilted her head and narrowed her eyes. "How do you feel? You're looking a bit peckish."

"I'm fine."

Another squinty examination, then a head shake. "I'm not sure you are. Did you eat something disagreeable at one of the coach stops yesterday? Do you think you picked up a parasite?"

Bile rose in her throat, but she swallowed it down.

Parasites? Of all the things to consider, that ranked toward the bottom of her list.

"That is truly revolting! Why, the very idea!" She dabbed at her right temple. "We were talking about whatever you're thinking about my being here. If you don't want me in your house, I'll move my things to the hotel."

She felt confident saying that now that they stood across from a rather nice building with a huge sign above its door proclaiming it to be the Wylder Hotel. If she had to relocate, at least the accommodations looked respectable.

"It's not that I don't want you. Of course I do. I have missed you, Daisy, and Pansy so very much it is fabulous to see the two of you again." She drew in a deep breath, then shrugged.

The other woman held her hands out, palms upward. "It's only that you seem so horribly unhappy, and you're spreading that unhappiness like a fever, sister. I know you must be wounded, after having your nuptials with Warren upended the way they were, but none of that is our fault. We are here to support you through this terrible time." She took a deep breath and gave a small stamp with one foot. "You needn't lash out at us because you're upset, though. It simply won't do!"

"Lash out? How can you say such a thing?" A rivulet of perspiration traced its way down her back. She wished the blue outfit were lighter. It hung heavy on her shoulders.

"Why, how can I not? You were rude when we picked you up, horrid to Lin when we got to my house, monstrously short-tempered when the accommodations weren't as lush as you hoped. Goodness gracious, Lily—can't you see you've been miserable since you arrived?"

Yes, she'd been wretched ever since Warren refused to marry her. What woman wouldn't be?

And if her gut were to be believed, she was about to be even more so.

She put a hand over her mouth, took the three steps from the porch at a run, and dashed around to the side of the building. She leaned over and hoped no one in this horrid town saw her lose the contents of her stomach in an embarrassing splatter at her feet.

Violet rubbed a hand on her back while she vomited, which should have made her feel better but instead brought tears to her eyes. Foolish, to cry like a child at being ill but she could not help herself.

"Don't cry." Her sister spoke in a soothing tone, handing her a fresh hanky perfumed with a hint of lavender. "Wipe your eyes, honey. You must have picked something up on the ride out here, is all. I bet a day or so of rest and you'll feel right as rain."

Chapter 10

Violet insisted Lily go straight to bed when they got back to her house. Having no strength to argue, she let herself be fussed over. It did not come naturally to her, being the first-born and usually the one fussing, but her sisters helped her undress, brought a jug of water and a clean glass for her bedside table, and put her to bed on the lumpy pillow in the tiny room.

Miraculously, she slept and when she woke her stomach felt much improved. Lying in bed, she wondered how long she'd slumbered. She ran a hand over her belly, hoping the indisposition had passed.

Had they been in Charleston she would have to hide her face in shame. Vomiting on a street the way she had—why, the memory of it made her twitch. Thankfully, no one she knew witnessed her indelicate moment. Even if someone saw, here in this untamed land vomit probably flew indiscriminately. They were most likely accustomed to bearing witness to such things.

Surely, that must be so. She hoped.

A light knock caught her attention. "Yes?"

The door opened and Violet entered carrying a wooden tray. "I hoped you'd be awake. How do you feel?"

"Better, thank you." She sniffed. "Something smells wonderful. What's in that bowl, sister?"

With a grin, the other woman set the tray down on the other bed. She lifted a napkin, spoon, and the bowl and brought them over. "Would you like me to feed you or do you feel strong enough to do it yourself?"

She held her hands out. "I can do it." Aromatic steam rose. The scent, a mix of carrots, potatoes, and leeks, filled her nose. She dipped the spoon, blew on the soup, and took a mouthful.

It tasted even better than it smelled.

Her sister sat on the other bed and watched her eat, her brow slightly furrowed.

"Stop worrying. I'm fine, really." She smiled between mouthfuls. "I think I had a touch of the ague, is all. Remember, you all had it once and I took care of you? Well, I believe my turn with the malady came— and at a most inopportune time. I am sorry I ended our little excursion to town in such a dreadful way."

The other woman relaxed a bit, letting her brow settle and mustering a smile. "We'll have time for lots of trips to town. I want you to feel better."

The truth came without hesitation. "I do. Much better."

"Good. I would hate to have to write Mother and tell her you arrived seriously ill—or that you took a bad turn on your first day here. Whatever would she think?"

"We don't want to worry her." The soup filled her with warmth. For the first time since she'd stepped off the stagecoach, she felt more herself. Strong, with a mind to taking charge of her circumstances again. She scooped up the last carrot and handed the bowl back. "Thank you. A nourishing soup."

Her sister put the lunch things on the tray with a nod. "I'll tell Lin you enjoyed it. She hoped you would."

The Chinese woman, again. Mother and Father would have conniptions if they knew one of their daughters shared a home with anyone, let alone a foreigner. Of all the sisters, Violet had always been the most accepting of every man, woman, and creature so it came as no surprise that she would form a friendship with the woman. But to have her in her house? That pushed the limits.

She straightened the bedclothes around her hips. "Oh, so she is your cook, then?"

Violet pulled her lips into a straight, thin line and her eyebrows came so close together that she looked as if a brown caterpillar walked across her forehead. Not a comely expression, at all.

"Lin is not my cook—she is my friend. More than that, even! I have already told you she and I are as close as sisters." She huffed a breath, stood, and lifted the tray. She turned and they locked gazes. "I meant what I said the day you arrived, Lily. If you can't respect the people in my life, you will not be welcome in my home."

She narrowed her eyes. "You're telling me that this Lin person would stay while you toss me out? Is that it?"

Her sister stood still for a long moment. Then, a nod. "That's exactly what I'm saying."

Chapter 11

Saturdays in Wylder weren't all cow rustlers and saloon brawls, as Lily expected.

By mid-afternoon her sister's house buzzed with activity.

Water heated and poured into a large, copper tub in the kitchen made for an abundance of lavender-scented steam. Each took a bath and since they began so early no one had to rush.

Violet insisted their newcomers bathe first. Daisy deferred to the eldest's position in the family so Lily went straight from bed to bath. Lingering in the fragrant water did wonders for her soul. She allowed Daisy to help with her hair and by the time the last suds had been rinsed she felt sure she'd been divested of pounds of western grime.

A roaring fire in the hearth in the front parlor warmed the room so well that she sat in comfort while her hair dried.

The room had a cozy, well-loved feel to it. The furnishings were simple, but tasteful. A settee with tables at either end, perfect for resting cups of tea or embroidery upon. A bit of stitching lay in progress on one table, proof of its usefulness. An overstuffed chair and footstool sat near the fire. Ginny, the cat, slept nestled against an armrest, as if it were a throne and she a queen.

Before a window, a table held knick-knacks. Not too many that they were cluttered but enough to see some charm in the humble home. Her sister's attention to detail impressed her. A small stack of books filled a basket beneath the table. Later, she would peruse the titles.

Daisy entered, wrapped in a robe, red-cheeked and smelling fresh from her bath. She sat on the footstool and gave the cat a soft pat before unwinding the towel from around her hair. Her locks cascaded across her shoulders, a divine shade of golden brown that sent a pang of jealousy to Lily's center.

The other woman shook her hair, then began finger-combing it to release snarls.

"My bones feel like tapioca, I'm so relaxed. I didn't realize I needed a proper bath until I slipped beneath the water." She sighed, shaking a tangle loose. "What about you? You must feel better now, don't you?"

She nodded. She did feel greatly improved, although tapioca had never been a favorite of hers.

"I do. And I agree, I needed a bath more than I imagined." She swept a hand to the room. "Violet has made quite a nice life for herself here. I'm surprised by that, too."

Her sister's fingertips were nearly ink-free. Now she waved one in the air and grinned. "You imagined she pitched a tent under a tree somewhere, surrounded by hostiles brandishing pistols, eating beans from a can, didn't you? Admit it, sister. That's exactly what you pictured."

She couldn't lie. Daisy came close to the truth. In her mind it had been succotash, not beans, but her theory fell close enough.

"Well, who could blame me? We hear such troubling news back home from the frontier. Why, I pictured our dear sister kidnapped by heathens or in such poor circumstances she'd be reduced to dancing on tables at the saloon. I'm glad that isn't the case."

The door opened and Violet came into the room. Lin followed. Both wore robes and had towel-wrapped heads.

"So am I." Violet smiled. "My dancing skills have never been as good as yours, Lily. I fear I'd dance my way right off the end of a table and break a leg!"

They all shared a giggle and in that moment it almost seemed they were back in Charleston, in the family home where they'd shared so many wonderful memories. Lily closed her eyes, imagined them pulled back in time. She smiled at the familiar laughter and allowed a hopeful spark to kindle inside her heart.

Chapter 12

Theo gave his niece a big grin as he reached out to smooth a hair back from her temple. Soon Alexia would be too old for an uncle's attention, so he didn't let this sweet moment in her childhood pass.

"You must've had quite a day." He dusted white powder off her skin and rubbed it between his fingertips. "Not only is your hair coming undone, but you're turning to dust right before my eyes."

The girl giggled and waved a hand at him. White covered two fingertips. "You're funny, Uncle. It's not dust—it's flour. Gertie is teaching me how to bake."

He raised his chin and sniffed the air. "I thought I smelled something."

"It's pumpkin bread. The recipe has a lot of stirring in it." She lowered her voice and leaned conspiratorially close. They were the only two in the front hallway, but she took care not to be overheard anyway. "Too much stirring, I think. Gertie insisted, so I kept at it. But Uncle, my arm is sore!" She ran a hand down her right arm and pulled a face.

Gertie, an older woman who lived next door to Thomas and Alexia, often stopped in to give the girl a woman's touch. Since Alexia's mother's death, a number of women attempted to take the dead woman's place, but the widower quickly sent them packing. The only one who had come with a mind to give a motherless child some love—with no thought to enticing the girl's father—had been the kindly neighbor.

She cooked many meals for the father and daughter, and never looked for compensation. The woman had a good heart, and the whole Harvey family, Theo included, adored her.

The sound of pots and pans clanging came from the kitchen. He lifted an eyebrow and tipped his head toward the far end of the hallway. "Shouldn't you be in there helping Gertie clean up? There must be bowls and spoons and…well, I don't know, things to scrub and put away."

The head bob loosened another tendril of auburn hair, but he let it dangle near her chin. Hard to believe time passed so quickly. It seemed they'd just celebrated this child's birth, yet here they were, and she stood closer to being a woman than a little girl.

Time moved from the beginning of life to the end without stopping. If he wanted to get himself settled with a wife, he needed to act fast. A wave of apprehension swept through him. Hell, but he hoped he hadn't wasted too much time.

"I'm going." She threw her arms around his waist and gave him a big hug. "I only wanted to see you for a minute. You are my favorite uncle, you know."

He looked down at her and grinned. "I'm your only uncle, sweet Alexia."

A shrug. "That, too." She released him and headed toward the kitchen but called over her shoulder before she rounded the corner. "When you and Father come home, stop in the kitchen. I'll leave pumpkin bread on the table for you."

"That sounds great, thank you."

Thomas came down the stairs. "What sounds great?"

"Pumpkin bread." He reached for his Stetson. A hat rack and wide mirror flanked the front doorway, so he glanced at his reflection before dropping the hat onto his head. "That's what she's baking with Gertie."

His brother snorted. "And don't I know it. I got a hug that smeared pumpkin on my other shirt. That's why I went upstairs to change." He glanced toward the kitchen. "Let's get out of here before she has a chance to do it again."

They stepped out onto the porch. The house sat on one of Wylder's more prestigious streets. Thomas' neighbors included an attorney and banker, as well as the widow with a baking talent. Rumor had it that Gertie inherited a fortune, but no one would know it by the humble lifestyle she led.

"You've given your daughter a nice home." He glanced at the two horses, saddled and waiting at the hitching post at the end of the front path. "It's respectable. A fine place to raise a family."

For a moment, the thought he should move into town tickled the corners of his mind. Maybe if he did, he'd be more likely to gain favor with a prospective wife.

Maybe Lily Bloom might consider him a suitor if he didn't live on the frontier.

The woman's beautiful blue gaze flashed in his head, a memory of a too-brief moment. How he'd wanted to lean close and wipe the grime from her alabaster skin…and then, simply take her in his arms and see if she remained as persnickety when someone held her close.

He liked starch in a woman. Also appealing, that she might melt given the right attention.

"Thanks. I like to think I'm doing right by Alexia." He paused, then went on in a somber tone. "I hope her mother approves."

Theo placed a hand on his brother's shoulder and gave him a squeeze. The man had been his hero since childhood, but that went even deeper now. How he'd survived such grief and moved on to find happiness for his daughter and with Violet seemed incomprehensible.

"Her mother does. I'm sure she's looking down on you both and smiling." Theo swallowed around the lump in his throat. "I can only imagine how that kind of love feels, and that deep loss. You're doing more than right by your girl, brother."

The other man took a deep breath. The evening had cooled and the scent from the flowers planted beside the front door sweetened the air.

"You'll feel that kind of love, too." Thomas met his gaze. "I know you will. I only hope you're spared the pain of losing her after you find her, is all."

"Me, too." He smiled, hoping to lighten the mood. "First, I have to find her."

They started down the steps.

"Oh, but I think you might've already found her. You've been preoccupied since that stagecoach rumbled into town, and that's a sure sign the woman's got your mind tangled up."

Theo stood beside his horse. A gentle bay, it remained still, and would do so for as long as he wanted. No impatient stomping or nickering, just a good, kind soul to journey forth with him. The characteristics he looked for when choosing horses were the same ones he valued in humans. That he found himself enamored with a woman who exhibited high-strung tendencies came as a surprise.

But he couldn't deny the attraction—or his brother's words. "You're right. My mind is tangled, and it began when Lily Bloom stepped off that coach."

The truth of it? The feeling of entanglement wasn't at all unpleasant. In fact, he rather liked the hold she had on him.

Chapter 13

"Are you ready to make new friends?" Daisy's eyes danced with delight at the prospect of having callers on their first Saturday night in town. Despite her bookish tendencies, she never balked at a social gathering, so Lily didn't find this out of character. "I can't wait. I bet they'll have some interesting stories to tell, and I for one am all ears!"

She yearned to be the cheery woman she'd been before Warren broke her spirit, so she forced a smile and nodded. Perhaps if she pretended to be happy it might happen. What could she lose by giving it a go?

"I am, actually. If we are to make a life here, the way Violet has done, we will need to get to know the locals." She stood before the looking glass in their shared bedroom. Her hair shone in the candlelight, so she tipped her head back and forth, admiring her clever updo and the way it shimmered. She patted her hair a final time before turning to her sister. "I hope they're somewhat civilized. I mean, this is the frontier, and you know there's more lawlessness here than anywhere else. I'm keeping my derringer in my pocket, and I advise you to do the same."

Before they left South Carolina, Father gifted each of his girls a pocket pistol—and made them vow to keep it on their person at all times. Lily hadn't wavered on that promise. The tiny over-under derringer nestled in a pocket, or if her skirt didn't have one, in her reticule, every day.

Now, she patted the side seam of her navy-blue skirt, relieved when the weapon bumped against her thigh.

The other pulled a face. "I'm not worried I'll be carried off by liquored-up rustlers or fall prey to some disreputable character right in my sister's home."

"You might be sorry. And we promised Father, remember." It fell to her to provide a good example for the others.

"Hmmph. What he doesn't know won't hurt him. Besides, you'll protect me, won't you?" She pointed to the tiny hole in the wall above the bed. "You've already practiced shooting, remember?" She smiled sweetly, then headed for the door. "Come on, let's get downstairs. We don't want the party to begin without us."

The stairs were narrow and steep, so Lily took care not to tumble down them. Recently she suffered a bout or two of lightheadedness. It would not do to fall now, not when she and the others had finally reached a level of companionability.

She heard male voices coming from the front parlor and there were hats lying with their brims up on the table beside the front door. She patted her hair one last time and smoothed a hand down the front of her skirt, then went into the parlor.

Standing beside the hearth, with their backs to her, stood two tall men. Both wore dark trousers and jackets. Their shoulders were broad, although the taller man appeared somewhat more muscled as the lines across the back of his jacket showed.

Violet looked up when Lily and Daisy reached the doorway. She held out a hand and said, "Why, there they are. Thomas, you met my sisters when the stagecoach came in a few days ago."

The man by her side turned and gave them a wide smile. "Ladies, it's good to see you again. I hope you're settling in nicely."

Her sister saved her the trouble of a reply. "Oh, we are, thank you. Lily and I are both feeling at home in Wylder already."

Their hostess put a hand on the other man's arm. "Lily and Daisy, I'd like you to meet Mister Theodore Harvey, Thomas' brother. Theo, these are my sisters, Lily and Daisy."

Daisy murmured a greeting, but Lily didn't hear the exchange. Her heart stuttered in her chest. The man cleaned up nicely, but she couldn't be fooled. A change of clothing, bath, and shave didn't turn a sow's ear into a velvet purse.

When he turned to face her, she inhaled sharply. If she were to make friends in this town she would have to swallow outbursts and keep her notions to herself, so she smiled and tilted her head.

"Miss Bloom." The same deep, silky voice she remembered. It sounded even more so now that it did not compete with rumbling wagon wheels, spirited saloon noise, or the bustle of street traffic. "I believe we had the pleasure of a brief, but meaningful, exchange when you stepped off the stagecoach. I hope you haven't forgotten that encounter."

"I have not, Mister Harvey."

Creases near the corners of his eyes appeared as if by magic when he grinned. His lightly bronzed skin, a testament to time spent outdoors she supposed, looked especially interesting when folded in upon itself. His eyes were dark brown, a shade that reminded her of expensive chocolate.

"I'm glad to hear it." He took a step closer when her two sisters and his brother began a conversation. When he drew near she tilted her head back, and realized how tall he stood. Of the four sisters, she topped the bunch and there were few who required her to gaze upward. That he did intrigued her. "I've been looking forward to seeing you again when I'm in a better condition. I apologize for appearing so rough the other day. I'd come into town after a night riding and I know I looked, ah…"

The devil sat on her shoulder, so she leaned close, lowered her voice, and offered, "Like the town drunk?"

The man didn't take offense. Instead, he tipped his head back and laughed, and the sound sent a burst of heat dancing low in her gut. He touched her somehow without ever placing a finger on her body, a sensation entirely new to her.

"Well, that's one way of putting it." He scrubbed a hand across his chin. "And I can't dispute your assessment. I'm sure I looked like I'd been dragged behind a bull across brush for a dozen miles. I probably smelled that way, too."

When she agreed to meet townspeople, in her heart she anticipated swearing miscreants, tobacco-stained and illiterate. This man did not fulfill her expectations, and it delighted her. Their conversation skipped along as lightly as if they were in Mother's parlor in Charleston.

"I fear I can't make any comment on your, um,

aroma. A good southern woman would never do such a thing." She glanced down, then back up to meet his gaze. "Mother would not be happy if one of her daughters were to offer an unseemly comment."

He leaned close and she caught a whiff of tobacco mixed with something spicy. A far cry from being hauled along by a wild animal.

"I understand and I appreciate that. I'm indebted to your mama for raising such charming daughters."

Heat rose within her, warming her cheeks. "I'll be sure to relay that sentiment when I write home."

Mister Harvey nodded his thanks. "I'd appreciate that. Now, tell me, Miss Bloom, how do you like our little town?"

She glanced over his shoulder. Her sisters, their Chinese houseguest, and the other Mister Harvey sat in a loose circle near the front window. The knick-knacks on the table had been cleared away, and now they shared a picture book. She watched them pass it around but did not bother to try to listen to their comments on whatever they viewed.

Did she like Wylder? How to answer, she wondered.

At home she would have given a reply she knew the man hoped for, regardless of what she truly felt. She'd been raised to do so, like other South Carolinian women. Seeming agreeable or content with whatever the world presented was expected, so she complied.

Now, though, she'd hit a crossroads in her life. Continue on, the way she'd always done—follow the path that brought her to this flight to the frontier? Those social standards had led her to this point, outcast from all she knew due to a man's stubborn strong will.

Or should she finally follow her own mind and heart? Do and say what came naturally instead of simply providing expected behavior?

Maybe Daisy had hit on something. Their parents were not present and couldn't dictate conduct or disparage any social infringement. She had no one to answer to save herself. No one to disappoint, either.

She met Mister Harvey's gaze. To his credit, he'd waited patiently while she weighed her options, neither pressing her nor losing interest. The expression in his eyes led her to believe he cared about her response but that had to be her imagination. Why should it matter to him?

As she opened her mouth, she chose which crossroad to travel.

"I must honestly say that I haven't seen enough of Wylder to know how I feel about the place." A finger of excitement ran up her spine. She'd spoken her mind, and the world had not stopped turning.

The man before her considered her words for a moment, then nodded. "That makes a lot of sense. You've barely arrived and while Wylder isn't a big place like Charleston, it still has a few interesting spots for newcomers to see."

That brightened her mood. Any points of significance in this dusty town were ones she needed to investigate.

"I'm glad to hear that. What would you consider the essential bits of town that a newly arrived person should look for?" Curiosity brought her a step closer. Suddenly she realized they still stood beside the fire. Neither had made a move to sit, they were so engaged in conversation. "Oh! Maybe we should sit?"

She led the way to the settee and sat toward one side. She'd left enough room for him. They were close enough to speak yet not so close their knees touched.

The man sat back against the cushions and rested an elbow on the padded armrest beside him. "Well, you were asking about the town's points of interest, weren't you?"

"Yes, please. If I'm to stay here I should acquaint myself with the sights." She imagined there might be three or four, aside from the ones that no respectable woman would want to see. She had no interest in locating saloons or, even worse, houses of ill repute. She'd chosen a crossroad, not a wrong turn toward decadence.

He tipped his head and studied her with a contemplative air. It sat fine with her that he hesitated because it gave her a moment to openly survey him, as well. His thick hair swept his jacket collar. Her fingers tingled. She wanted to reach out and touch the locks to see whether they were as soft as they appeared.

"Well, it would seem to me that a newcomer should engage a guide. You know, someone familiar with the area who's able to show a person where to go, what to see, and even who to trust." He held out a hand between them. "Because, you know, not everyone is as trustworthy as I am."

She smiled, amused by his charm. "Is that so?"

"It is." A nod to punctuate the point.

"So you're telling me you're the man to trust?"

He nodded again. "I am, indeed, a man who is certainly honorable. Ask my brother. I'm sure he'll vouch for me."

She looked over to where the others sat. They still

passed around a book and were discussing the photos on the pages. The gathering seemed comfortable, as if they were at ease in Violet's home.

Her sister really had made a good life for herself. Of course, she'd arrived in Wylder to find her intended lying in the town cemetery, but at least she had gotten this house. Nothing like their family home, but it would do.

The best part? She seemed genuinely content. Her position at the school, the gentleman seated beside her, new friends…all things to be proud of.

Her younger sister's life turned out better than her own. A pang of envy sliced her, but she chased it away. Her life hadn't reached its peak yet. Still time to find the kind of happiness Violet had.

"Your brother will vouch for you? But how do I know he's reliable?"

Mister Harvey lowered his voice enough that she leaned closer to hear him. "I'll guarantee his upstanding position but don't let on. I don't want his head to grow too fat for his hat, if you know what I mean."

Lily couldn't help the laughter that bubbled up from somewhere deep within her. The man's charm captivated her in a most unexpected way.

"Well, what do you have in mind?" She held her breath, hoping he would suggest the very same thing she had in her own head.

"It would please me to show you around Wylder tomorrow." He smiled hopefully. "Sunday is a fine day to stroll on Wylder Street. It's about as peaceful a time as this town has, and I think you might get a favorable impression of things without all the comings and goings of a weekday."

For the first time in a long time, something had gone her way.

"I'd like that very much, Mister Harvey."

Chapter 14

Sundays in Charleston were far better than those in the Wyoming territory, she decided. It must be the air or perhaps the dust, but Lily woke feeling nauseated and not at all like seeing the town with Mister Harvey.

Still, she forced herself to wash and dress. While the idea of food turned her stomach, she did manage to make it downstairs. She sat in the parlor, beside the cold hearth, and pulled a blanket around her shoulders.

The Chinese woman appeared on silent feet. She stood in the doorway, her hands folded near her waist, and tilted her head. "You feel okay? No mean to intrude but you look very pale."

Lily hadn't spoken with the other woman yet and she'd assumed she didn't speak English well. But her attention to pronunciation made every word understandable.

She had to give the woman recognition for learning a foreign language.

"I'm fine, thank you." She swallowed hard as a cold sweat broke out along her hairline. "It is very kind of you to ask."

The woman came into the room and stood a few feet from the settee. Her gaze probed Lily's, making it difficult to concentrate on not being ill. She threw the blanket aside, heat making her perspire.

"You do not look fine. Not fine at all."

Obstinate refusal to embarrass herself again made her stick to denying the truth. She hated any kind of infirmity or weakness. How could she succumb to either now?

"I. Am. Fine." Every word came with effort as the room began to spin.

"Not fine." The Chinese woman came close enough to place the back of her hand against Lily's forehead. "Not hot. But sticky. Very sticky." She leaned down and they locked gazes. "Green. Very green."

As Lily's stomach began to contract, the other woman grabbed the discarded blanket and held it beneath her chin. A slow hand rubbed her back as she got sick and soothing words reached her ears, accompanying the horrid retching sounds coming from within her. She had no idea what the other woman said but it did not matter. She hadn't been left alone in her moment of suffering. The kindness wouldn't be forgotten.

She hadn't eaten since the night before so little more than bile rose. When the retching ended, the other wiped Lily's chin with an edge of the blanket, folded it up, and walked to the door.

"Will bring a cup of tea." She looked back over her shoulder. "You sit. No move."

She nodded, too wrung out to speak, thinking that just like that, the eldest Bloom sister took directions from a Chinese woman. Who would have ever believed it could happen?

She lay back against the settee, dropped her head toward the ceiling, and waited for the shakes to pass. The funny thing about it, as soon as she vomited she felt better. The same thing happened yesterday.

What kind of ailment brought these strange symptoms? She had an idea, but it couldn't be that. No, it didn't merit contemplating—it couldn't be. She simply hoped this passed quickly. She had no time for fussing with sickness.

She lifted her head when she smelled mint.

"Thank you, Lin." She accepted the teacup and saucer from the other woman. "I'm grateful for your help."

A nod, then, "Thank you, too."

She took a sip of tea. Warm, minty, and with a hint of sweetness, it slid down her throat in a soothing wave. "Why are you thanking me? You're the one who took care of me when I fell ill. I didn't do anything for you—in fact, I gave you a rather messy blanket, I'm afraid."

Lin sat in a chair near the hearth. A petite woman with a long, black braid falling over her shoulder, she wore a fashionable navy-blue ensemble. Despite the outfit, a beautifully exotic air surrounded her.

"Thank you, Miss Bloom. For the first time, you speak with me. You use my name." She placed a hand on her chest above her heart. "In my beloved China, this is sign of respect. I am thankful."

Shame threatened to upend her gut again, so she took another sip of tea and considered her reply. Her actions toward the other woman had been deplorable, tinged by her own unhappiness as well as the intolerance for those who were different, a trait she inherited from her parents.

Lily swallowed her pride. She placed the cup and saucer on the edge of the table beside her and met the other's gaze. "I have not behaved well since my arrival.

68

I apologize for being so horrid, Lin. Please forgive me."

A smile lifted the corners of the rosebud-pink lips high. "It is a long trip."

"Yes, it is but that's no excuse. I'm so sorry." Behind her eyes, prickles that made her blink. How had her emotions come on so quickly? Whatever had happened to her?

"We are fine, Miss Bloom. No need to be sorry any longer." Kindness suffused every word, making the prickling sensations in her eyes worse.

"We aren't fine." She dashed a fingertip beneath her right eye and caught a tear before it fell. "You must call me Lily, please. No formalities. I believe we've crossed the line from strangers to friends."

Lin smiled so sweetly her whole face lit up. A decisive nod. "Lily. A very beautiful name."

Chapter 15

Theodore Harvey's rugged appeal intrigued Lily in a way she couldn't quite put a finger on. Now that he'd cleaned up—nicely, too—and had shown himself to be something other than the town drunk, she saw him in a new light.

A knock alerted her, so she smoothed a hand over her skirt, checked her hairpins were firmly affixed, and walked over to the front door. She pulled it open—and found not one, but two visitors.

Mister Harvey stood on the porch looking as shiny as a freshly minted silver dollar. He wore dark brown jacket, vest, and slacks. The sharp crease in his trousers and the still-damp shine on his hair when he removed his hat showed he'd taken some care to present himself in a favorable manner.

He held his Stetson loosely at his side, tipped his head, and smiled. "Good afternoon, Miss Bloom. You're looking mighty pretty in that color. Matches your eyes right nice."

Heat crept up her chest, touching her neck and finally, her cheeks.

When he glanced down at the neckline of her dress, she grew hotter still. The cut, to the latest eastern fashion, plunged a bit more than most dresses seen out here in the west. The swell of her breasts rose and fell with each breath, apparent to any who cared to witness the action. That she'd worn the dress with Warren, and had caught his attention, crossed her mind when she dressed for this day's outing.

She'd hoped to catch the man's interest. That she did filled her with satisfaction.

"Why, you are very kind, Mister Harvey. And does it? Match my eyes, that is?" She gazed up into his face and fluttered her lashes.

"It sure does, ma'am." When the child beside him shifted from foot to foot, he cleared his throat and put a hand on the girl's shoulder. "This is my niece, Alexia. She's Thomas' daughter." He gazed down at the girl and gave her a tender smile before returning his gaze to meet Lily's. "We figured this is a good chance for us all to become better acquainted. Living in Wylder, you're going to see a lot of this young lady."

The girl looked fourteen or so. Long, auburn hair tied back with a blue-and-white checked ribbon. The sash on her dress matched, and all the shades of blue in her outfit blended seamlessly. No doubt the ensemble had been handmade, and likely cost a pretty penny.

Well, then. Good to know that Violet kept company with a man of means.

She gazed at the brother standing before her. Did he, too, have a sizeable bank account?

Turning her attention on his niece, she held out a hand, delighted when the girl offered hers in return. They did not shake, merely held hands for a companionable moment before breaking contact. "I'm pleased to meet you, Alexia. I met your father already. He seems like a very nice man."

The girl dipped her chin. "Pleased to make your acquaintance, ma'am. Yes, my father is a good man."

"He's friends with my sister, I hear."

A small grin. "Oh, yes. They're special friends. Miss Bloom—the other one, not you—she's my teacher at the school. I have a feeling that's why Father hasn't asked her to marry him yet."

Lily raised a brow. "Ah, is that so? Does your father not think schoolteachers make good wives?"

The girl giggled, holding a hand beside her cheek. "I don't know about that. I think he doesn't want to make it awkward for me, is all. You know, having my new mother be my teacher."

Her uncle cleared his throat again. Lily met his gaze, and they shared a quiet smile.

He held out an arm. "Miss Bloom? Are you ready to see some of Wylder before we head over to Thomas' place for dinner?"

Pulling the door closed with one hand, she nodded and placed the other on his arm. "I am. And I would like that very much."

They'd driven over in a sporty two-wheeled trap. Its sleek style made it ideal for excursions, such as afternoon jaunts. A beautiful black horse waited patiently in the sunshine.

A small step ladder unfolded from its side so Alexia climbed up with ease. When her turn came, she accepted the man's offer of assistance. His broad hand swallowed hers and his steadying strength made finding her way to the seat a snap. When she settled beside the girl, he flipped up the steps and went around to the other side.

Three fit comfortably on the narrow wooden seat. With the girl between them, it could hardly be considered a romantic outing but there would, hopefully, be time later for her to get closer to the man. That he interested her at all after the unfortunate circumstances of her breakup made her hopeful. Maybe she would find happiness in Wylder, after all.

"Do you like horses, Miss Bloom?" The girl gazed up at her with sparkling eyes. Lily noticed they were the clearest blue, a perfect match for such an outfit as the one she wore. "Do you ride?"

She had learned to ride at an early age. All the sisters had at Father's insistence.

"I do. Am I correct in guessing you like horses, too?"

"Oh, yes! Dearly!" Her hands clutched near her heart, she bounced in the seat. "Father promised to buy me my own horse. He's talking with Mister Holt—he's the man to go to if you want a quality piece of horseflesh, that's what Father says. They haven't found a horse for me yet, but I know she'll be perfect when they do."

"If you don't mind, we're taking my horse-loving niece to the livery. She'll be able to get her fill of horses for the day, before we drop her off at Thomas'." He glanced down at the girl and said, "Where she's promised to help Violet, Lin, and Daisy ready the meal and set the table."

The livery came into view, sending an ear-to-ear smile across their young companion's face. "Yes, that's right. I'm to go home and help, but first I get to see the horses. Maybe I can feed one an apple." She reached into her pocket and pulled out a piece of fruit. "I brought my own, you see. In case there aren't any at the livery."

"Good to plan for things." She looked over to the

man holding the reins. "And you, Mister Harvey? Have you brought a treat for the horses, as well?"

He pulled back, and the horse stopped. Before he jumped down, he met her gaze and nodded. "I have. I've brought a lovely lady wearing a dress that matches her pretty eyes. That's enough of a treat for anyone on a Sunday afternoon."

Chapter 16

The livery enchanted the girl. She spoke to each horse in its stall and, to her absolute delight, assisted in grooming an especially gentle mare.

The man turned to Lily and held an arm toward the open door at the far end of the barn. "Would you care to see the horses in the fenced area out back? It's a pleasant view of the hills beyond town and there's a bench where we might rest."

"That sounds wonderful."

They made their way through the barn. The floor was swept clean and the stalls looked tidy, too. She tucked the details away in her mind. The owner did right by these animals. If she ever had cause to board a horse, this would be her top choice.

Mister Harvey stopped to rub the nose of a large Appaloosa. It nickered and stamped a foot in greeting.

"She seems to know you. Is this your animal?" She reached out hand and smoothed it over the horse's head.

"Stardust is mine. I keep her here when I'm in town." He rubbed the horse between its eyes. "Nothing but the best for my gal."

They turned back and covered the few feet remaining. She stopped in the doorway, overtaken by the sweeping vista. She'd given no thought to finding any beauty out here. This expanse of green leading up to craggy brown mountains, beneath the cloudless blue sky, enchanted her.

"It's so beautiful." The words came out on a sigh. "I never dreamed it would be this way."

He stood beside her and for a long moment they gazed to the distance.

"What did you expect when you moved out here? You must've known it wouldn't be like Charleston." He glanced down at her and raised a corner of his lip. He grew handsomer when he teased her. "You did know that, didn't you?"

That jesting came naturally between them shocked her. She did not take as smoothly to the lighter parts of life, the way her sisters did. The responsibility of being the eldest sat firmly in her mind, making her feel her attitude should be of a serious nature. It fell to her to be an example for the others, and how could she do that if she giggled and joked all the time?

She couldn't. So she didn't. But now, in this new environment standing beside this kind man, it felt right. Comfortable, even.

A firm mental shove pushed thoughts of duty and the past from her head. A new opportunity presented itself and she'd be a fool to let it pass.

"Yes, I knew that! Goodness, I'm from the east, not a pumpkin patch."

Raking his gaze from her face to her feet and then back up again, he shook his head. "I never would've taken you for a pumpkin, believe me."

He amused her in a way no man ever had. She gave in to the urge and laughed. It had been so long since she'd done so it felt both strange and refreshing.

"You have a beautiful laugh." He met her gaze with a smoldering stare that brought goosebumps up on her arms.

"Why, you're too kind."

"Thank you but I didn't say it to flatter you. It's the truth—your laughter is like rain falling on a metal roof. Soothing and sweet, filled with promise." He rubbed a hand across his chin and squeezed one eye closed. "I need to learn to shut my mouth. Now I've probably embarrassed you."

She felt a lot of things running around inside her heart, mind, and body but embarrassment was not one of them.

"I'm flattered by the thought—no one has ever said such sweet things to me but more than that I'm grateful you feel comfortable speaking the truth as you see it. I think we need more of that."

He held out his arm, so she put her hand near his elbow. They walked to a low, backless wooden bench near a watering trough. When they sat the view of the hills gave a different perspective. More green, less brown, but equally enchanting.

"So you're a woman who likes the truth? Pardon me, but that's a bit unusual, isn't it?"

She could have taken offense but did not. The day progressed too well to let him unsettle her. "Whatever do you mean, Mister Harvey? Explain yourself, please." She added a smile so he could not feel she asked because he'd crossed a line.

"Why, it's been my experience that most women prefer to hear a softened tale, if you will." He ran a hand down the thigh of his trousers before he held it out, palm up as if offering his words on a tray. "Will the snowstorm be horrid? No, a passing squall, no need to worry. Might bandits come upon us while we sleep?

No, of course not, we are perfectly safe. Does this dress make my figure look wide? Oh, certainly not! It is charming!"

He grinned when he finished and for the second time in less than an hour, she laughed. This time, Lily let her head fall back and she didn't hold herself in check for modesty's sake.

"Mister Harvey! I do declare, you are witty and entertaining. I see now that you do have a point— women never want to hear that their figures are less than svelte or that they'll be besieged by bandits and snow squalls."

"I'm glad you understand." He hesitated a moment, looking hard into her eyes. "It might be bold of me to ask but do you think you could call me Theo? Mister Harvey makes me think my father is approaching."

Back home in Charleston, that would never do. But she wasn't there now and calling him by his given name seemed less tedious by far, so she nodded.

"Thank you. I'm glad you're not offended."

She shook her head. "Not at all. I appreciate your honesty, Mister—um, Theo."

"We could make a pact." He looked toward the hills, then back at her. "To tell each other the truth, at all times."

Lily mulled the thought over. It would be refreshing to have a friend to confide in, someone who wasn't a sister and therefore didn't need her to present a good example. The lure of being unapologetically herself with someone proved too much to resist.

She nodded. "I like that pact so yes, I agree we should be honest with each other, always. But that means you won't tell me my figure is fine if I ask if my bustle makes my hips look wide, remember."

He placed a hand above his heart. "I promise to be truthful about your hips at all times."

Her nod came with a smile now—and that, being unexpectedly happy—made her beam inside, too. "It's nice we got that settled. But there is one more thing we should discuss."

"And that is?"

"Well, if I call you by your given name, and we have such a dear friendship that we are honest at all times, perhaps you should use my given name, also. Besides, with Daisy and Violet in town, there are already too many Miss Blooms to keep track of."

Theo chuckled. "I see your point. As you wish, Lily."

"Good. So, we are quickly becoming friends, it seems." Warmth filled her so fully she pulled in a deep breath. The scent of horses, grass, and something sweeter came on a wave of peace. "I admit, I need one."

"It's hard to move to a new place, even if you do have some family there. But don't fret, you'll find your way." He paused and shot her a huge grin. "Especially now that you've got both a guide and companion."

"I'm sure you're right. So what's on our—"

The sound of running footsteps coming from inside the barn stopped her. She turned to see what went on but before she swiveled her head a mass of flapping feathers landed on her lap.

"Uncle Theo, look! It's a—" Alexia's tone changed from joy to panic. "No, wait—she's gotten away!"

"Oh!" Lily rushed to stand as chicken claws dug into her skirt. One pierced the fabric and found her thigh. She wrapped her arms around her face as she stood. "Get it off me!"

Theo's body brushed hers as he made a grab for the fowl the same moment the young girl dashed over to reclaim her surprise. Between the chicken, grabbing man, grasping girl, and her own fear, Lily lost her balance and tumbled backward—and splashed right into the trough!

The water was much colder than she thought it would be and the dress soaked up liquid at an alarming rate.

The chicken flew off.

Chapter 17

Her ruined dress dripped water into a puddle at their feet in Theo's trap. That he didn't say a word about the mess raised him even higher in her regard.

He maneuvered the horse down side streets rather than the main roads where everyone would see her dishevelment. When they reached Violet's house, he held a hand up to help her exit.

The small step proved slippery when she placed a wet sole on it. Her foot slid and she pitched forward— and would have fallen into the street if not for the quick-thinking man.

"Oh!" The sound escaped her throat without conscious effort.

His hands wrapped around her waist as her face landed on his shoulder. The scent of tobacco and clean man swept up her nose. His hair tonic had a bit of mint to it that made her mouth water.

"Steady, there. We don't need you to take another tumble. One is more than enough for any day." He held her close, perhaps a moment longer than absolutely necessary, before he dropped her feet to the ground and released her.

"Thank you." She ran a hand over her hair. It had survived the dunking, but her hat had been sacrificed for it. Meeting his gaze, she shrugged. "I know I look a sight."

He put a hand beneath her left elbow, and they walked toward the house. "You look, as ever, beautiful. Come on, let's get you inside and out of those wet clothes."

A shiver ran through her. He couldn't mean to help her undress, could he?

Then it hit her. Without a sister or servant nearby, could she unfasten the buttons on the back of her dress on her own? Especially now that they were encased in sopping wet fabric?

The house seemed eerily quiet without any of the others within to liven it up. She placed her reticule on the table inside the door. It had luckily not been submerged.

They looked at each other then. Where to begin?

She couldn't very well try to go upstairs with sodden shoes, not after they showed how prone to slipping they were. Yet how could she remove them here under the man's watchful eye?

He took matters in hand and for once it relieved her to allow someone else the task.

"Come, sit down on the step." He pointed to the staircase. The pine risers were varnished so her wet skirt would not harm them. "Let's get your shoes off so you don't slip again."

What could she do?

She sat, and like a small child allowed the man to remove her shoes. He did so with care, reaching beneath the hem of her skirt without exposing her legs.

"Thank you for helping me." Heat bloomed in her cheeks when his hand brushed her right calf. His touch, soft and gentle, brought warmth to her chilled skin. "I don't know how I'd manage on my own."

One shoe hit the floor, so he reached for the other leg. Again, he swept a finger on her skin as he tucked it beneath the upper edge of her shoe and began to tug at the buttons.

"That's what friends are for." He took a deep breath and lifted his gaze to hers. "I still can't apologize enough for my niece and that chicken. I'm as shocked as you are and I'm so sorry."

If she thought about it too much her blood boiled so she pushed it from her mind. Well, almost.

"It's not your fault." She paused and pulled her lips into a tight line while she considered her next words. Meaningful conveyance without a sarcastic edge had never been a strong point for her. And they had promised to be honest with each other, after all. "But she's at an age where she shouldn't be chasing chickens, Theo. It's not seemly. And if she hadn't been doing so, well we wouldn't be here, would we?"

She ran a hand down the front of her skirt. They both grimaced when the fabric made a squelching noise.

The second shoe came away from her foot, so he placed it near the wall. Then he reached for the first shoe and lined it beside the other.

"I'm not sure if you're aware but Alexia's mother is dead. My brother does a good job raising her, but I admit, some of the things a mother might teach are lacking." He gave her a small smile. "But Violet is standing in well, actually. For both Thomas and my niece. If she weren't so busy at the schoolhouse she might be able to spend even more time with them. And then maybe my dear girl might not be so enamored with chickens."

She shivered. The fabric felt clammy against her skin.

But a question nagged her mind since she arrived in town.

"Why aren't they married? I mean, they've been keeping company for a while and from the looks they give each other they're compatible. So why not tie the knot and be done with it?"

Theo's eyebrows rose but he met her gaze without flinching.

"Well, you do get right to the heart of things, don't you?"

"We promised to be honest with each other, remember?" She pulled her lips into a smile even though her teeth were close to chattering. "He's your brother so I assume you know what's on his mind."

He still knelt at her feet and made no move to rise.

"I expect I know his heart. Hers, too. I think they love each other but are waiting for Alexia's sake." He ran a hand through his dark locks and shook his head. "Me, I wouldn't do it that way, but we all travel our own paths."

"What do you mean? How would you do it differently?"

She thought waiting for the girl to be comfortable with a replacement for her mother a kindness. As she didn't fall into syrupy sentimental actions too often, that she did think it the considerate move came as a mild shock. Not her typical hard-edged reality way of seeing situations, for sure. Maybe the trip west softened her some. Who could tell? At any rate, she didn't see the harm in finding compassion for the girl.

He sat back on his heels and crossed his arms over

his chest. "You want the uncoated truth?"

She nodded, not trusting her voice. A chill swept through her and she hoped his explanation came quickly.

"We're living in hard times, in a rough place. Settling the frontier doesn't come easy and even in towns like Wylder there are perils." He stopped and took a deep breath. "I think that time wasted can never be recalled. This isn't Philadelphia, where I'm from, or your home, Charleston. Here, we need to take what we can get, satisfaction-wise, and make the best of it. That goes for everything, including the goings on between men and women."

She saw merit in his words. They echoed the sentiment she felt with regard to Warren, the one he hadn't shared. If they'd moved forward and made the best of things, had some backbone about their hardships, they'd have found some way to make a life together. She felt sure of it.

But that ship had sailed. Now she would never know if she and her once-betrothed would have found happiness.

"You probably think I should be more romantic about it." He shot her a small grin. "I know that's how women feel, that there should be flowers and sweet talk instead of involving the harsh realities of western life."

She shook her head and pushed up from the step. "N-n-not at all." Her teeth chattered as the cold fabric sucked onto her form like a second skin. "I q-quite agree."

Theo ran a hand down her arm and scowled. "Whatever are we doing talking this way? You're chilled to the bone! We need to get you into some warm clothes."

He placed his arms beneath her and lifted her, so she lay against his chest. Without asking for permission, he began to climb the stairs. At the top, he paused and looked at the doorways.

"Which one?"

She pointed to the tiny room she shared with Daisy. He walked in and set her down on her feet. Then, he turned her, so she faced away from him and began to undo the buttons running down the back of her dress.

"T-t-that isn't—"

He didn't let her finish. "It's necessary. It's bad enough I allowed my niece's chicken friend to fly at you so you fell into a horse trough. I can't let you catch your death, too."

The sides of her dress fell away from her shoulders and instantly she didn't feel nearly as cold and damp. The fabric weighed so much that without it her body grew lighter.

He pushed the dress off her shoulders and helped her wiggle out of it. When it hit the floor with a soggy thud he leaned down while she stepped out of it.

Theo stood and their gazes locked. Clad only in her undergarments she should have been mortified—yet she wasn't. Not one bit. A shiver passed through her and it had nothing to do with damp clothing. It heated her from inside, sending warmth pooling in her center.

Suddenly the chill on her skin left and her teeth stopped chattering. She forgot the physical distress the dunking had wrought and the only thing that mattered, the sound of his breathing mingling with hers, filled her mind.

She leaned closer and tilted her head up a fraction of an inch.

His gaze dropped to her lips, where it lingered for a long moment. When he closed the distance between their faces ever so slightly her breath caught. She imagined what his lips on hers would feel like and lowered her eyelids halfway in anticipation.

The sound of his throat clearing brought her back to the present moment.

"I'm concerned you'll catch a chill if we stand here much longer."

Her voice came out as a whisper. "Thank you."

He nodded. To his credit, he didn't drop his gaze. "You're welcome. Do you need more help?" He swallowed, then added, "Or should I take this dress downstairs and wait for you?"

"That would be best, I think."

He turned and walked through the door. She heard his bootheels on the stairs. In the empty little house she heard him move through the rooms.

When he reached the kitchen, she released the breath she held.

No matter how they'd agreed to be truthful with each other she could not admit to him that she had been sorely tempted to ask him to help her remove the rest of her garments. Or that disappointment filled her now that she hadn't done so.

Chapter 18

Lily found Theo waiting on the front porch. He sat on a bench looking out onto the street. Sunday afternoon foot traffic offered a lively view.

He stood when she opened the door and waited while she crossed the floor. She sat, motioning with a tip of her head toward the space beside her so he resumed his place.

"How do you feel? Are you feeling poorly? I can fetch Coyote if you think it's necessary."

She tightened her fingers on the light blue wrap she'd draped over her shoulders. It, like her dress, matched the ribbons on the toes of her shoes.

"Is it customary to bring a wild animal to cure temperature fluctuations out here in the west? Why at home we'd run for a hot water bottle, not a coyote."

A grin turned concern to amusement and her knees to water. Oh, but the man had a handsome smile!

"Coyote is Wylder's doctor. Some call him Doc Sullivan but most of us go by his nickname." He tapped his hat on his knee. "And before you ask me about that, I have no idea at all why he's called Coyote. I figure every man is entitled to a secret or two and that one's all his."

"Well, that makes sense. I thought you were considering wrapping me in some living, furry animal. I wondered how quickly I could get in the house and close the door on that suggestion!" She smiled, then shook her head. "And thank you, but no, I don't need a doctor. I feel fine."

That half-truth seemed to satisfy him.

Her gut danced a bit, but not nearly as badly as it had these past days. Still, the idea of a full Sunday meal put her off.

"Glad to hear that." He waved to a man in a passing buckboard before he turned to face her. His gaze warmed her and for an instant she forgot her belly. "Now I know what you had in those trunks that came in on the stage with you."

A brow lifted but she kept her lips closed and waited for him to continue.

"They were filled with pretty baby-blue dresses, weren't they? Just about every time I've seen you, you're wearing a dress that matches those beautiful eyes." He paused and gave a thoughtful glance toward the street. When he met her gaze his eyes shimmered. "I have to admit, it's one of the things I miss about being so far from home."

"How so?" That he yearned for home so thoroughly that it nearly brought tears to his eyes pulled at her heartstrings. The man's intensity touched her as if he'd placed a hand on her chest.

"In the east, women dress like women. I understand and appreciate some women here need to wear working clothes, to help on homesteads or ride, but on a Sunday afternoon a woman should look…well, as pretty as a picture. And you, Lily, are the most beautiful picture I have ever seen."

Speechlessness did not come over her often but at this instant every rational thought flew from her head.

Her eyes rounded and she wondered if she looked like a startled duck, but she could not help herself.

The man touched her in ways she didn't dream possible.

A fine sheen touched her temples. She wiped the back of one hand across her skin and pushed her hair back, even though the pins kept it in place. One last pat to the smooth locks as she searched for a response.

Had she been in South Carolina, a giggle and airy wave would do. Men were satisfied with the fine art of casual flirtation there. In fact, she suspected they expected it. Here, though, life felt more substantial to her, as if an added layer of meaning covered every dusty exchange.

"Why, I hardly know what to say." She ran a finger across her upper lip. The heat did make a woman shimmer. "You're so kind. But I must admit, I honestly feel as if I'm melting in this heat."

His brow creased.

Then, he did something entirely unexpected. He reached out a hand and placed his wrist against her forehead.

"I'm not sure I shouldn't go for the doctor. You're looking awful pale." He took his wrist away and ran a slow finger down the side of her face, sliding it across her temple until he held her chin in his hand. "No blazing fever, you're nice and cool, but I'm concerned you did catch a chill."

He could be concerned about whatever he wanted as long as he kept his hand on her face. Warmth spread from his touch and for the first time since she'd left Charleston hope surged within.

"No chill, I promise." She leaned her chin into his

hand when he started to pull away. They sat joined for the most glorious seconds before Theo drew back and placed his hand on his knee. "I think I'm a bit overwhelmed by the change, is all. The long trip, then adjusting to life in the west."

"I understand that. It's a lot to take in and while it would seem that you'd have time to contemplate the move during the trip, a bouncing coach is no place for quiet contemplation, is it?"

She shook her head. "It's not. What a miserable way to travel!"

He winked. "And then, you arrive and find the town drunk waiting to greet you…"

Laughter bubbled up from inside her. Her first impression had been exactly that. No denying it so she reached for his face and ran a hand over his chin.

That she touched him so familiarly shocked them both.

That his face felt smooth and warm set her fingertips on fire, but in a wonderful way that made her breath catch. Theo didn't move when she traced his jawline with her index finger or smoothed her palm across his cheek.

"What could I think? You were covered with stubble and looking kind of ragged…nothing like you do now." She spoke softly, then pulled her hand away. As soon the contact between them ceased she missed it.

"Good point. I didn't look too respectable, at that. But you, well, you were just as lovely even with that slash of trail grime across your beautiful face."

Theo leaned so close she caught a whiff of peppermint from his breath.

When his mouth claimed hers she didn't resist. His

lips were smooth and pressed against hers so tenderly that every thought flew from her mind.

When he angled his face to deepen the kiss, she wondered if this was what heaven felt like.

Time really did stand still when one fell into another's arms because she had no idea how long they kissed, only that she didn't want it to end.

The thump of footsteps on the wooden flooring brought them apart.

Lily opened her eyes and swiveled her head so quickly she gave herself a crick in her neck.

Thomas and Violet stood three feet away.

Her sister's eyebrows were so far up they came close to hiding in her hair. And Thomas? He grinned from ear to ear, obviously amused by the display.

Crossing her arms across her chest, the other woman heaved a deep sigh. "Well, I suppose we worried needlessly. You're obviously none the worse for the wear after having gone for a swim in the horse trough at the livery. I'm glad you're, ah, recovered."

Chapter 19

Lily stood with her face turned toward the cloudless blue sky and let the sun's warm fingers caress her cheeks. She knew she shouldn't. Risking her creamy complexion this way would send Mother into fits—but Mother remained in Charleston and the sun and sky were oh, so mesmerizing.

Besides, no one watched. For once, she managed to prepare for an outing before the others. Well, before Daisy, anyway.

Violet taught today so she left for the schoolhouse almost before dawn.

Lin hurried out right after breakfast, murmuring something about an appointment with a shop owner. She hadn't gotten the gist of the woman's explanation, only that it held a place of importance and couldn't be missed.

She and her young sister were left alone in the snug little house for the morning. They'd tidied up, then she read while the other scribbled in her book. It had been a peaceful time, almost the first quiet moments the pair shared since their arrival in Wylder.

Perhaps they were both settling into this western lifestyle.

If she didn't find her way here, she had no idea what she would do—or where she could go. Returning to Charleston was unthinkable. Everyone there must know by now why her wedding had been cancelled. For all she knew, Warren had jawed with his cronies and, to increase his own self-esteem, disclosed he'd had his way with her. She didn't trust him any further than she could heave him. No man who claimed a woman's virginity before casting her aside deserved trust.

"Well, look at you, keeping your face to the sun and letting shadows fall behind you." Daisy's heels tapped on the wooden steps as she descended. She stopped beside her and tipped her face upward, too. A few seconds passed before she said, "You know Mother would have our heads for this. She'd be pouring buttermilk baths for both of us and telling us we're bound to look like old crones before we reach thirty."

"Oh, you know our mother well. That's exactly what she'd say." She gave in to the surprising impulse to giggle. "Why, right about now she'd be near a conniption fit over this. Well, it's a good thing she can't see us. And remember that she always means well, even when she's dunking one of us in buttermilk-filled bathtubs!"

Her sister met her gaze and grinned. "Yes, that's a fact. But truly, Lily, you look very content, almost like a cat who's sipping at the milk itself. Wylder agrees with you, I think."

They draped their reticules over their wrists, checked their hats were secure, and set off for the main part of town. Violet's house, set on a residential street, sat near enough to the heart of things that they didn't need a buggy. A short, pleasant walk on a bright spring day brought a smile to her face.

She mulled over the other woman's words.

Aside from the persistent queasiness in her belly,

she did feel satisfied.

"I believe you're right, actually. I think the situation in Charleston wore away at me." She took a deep breath when the memory of Warren's hateful behavior forced its way into her mind. With a scowl, she added, "That man—it's good to have some distance between us, at that."

"He broke your heart, then?"

Of all the childish, fanciful thinking.

"You spend too much time penning wildly romantic stories, sister. Real life isn't all rainbows and roses, you know. And not everyone who agrees to marry is in love with the one they've promised to wed." She gave a sniff. The closer they got to Wylder Street, the more dust floated in the air. So many horses, too, made breathing deeply impossible. "He did not break my heart, I assure you. He broke a bargain we'd made and that is where the disappointment comes in."

They passed a number of shops but did not stop in any of them. Monday morning brought out lots of townsfolk. She imagined how it might feel to know some of the faces by name. A few nodded greetings but none stopped them, which suited her fine. No time to talk, anyhow.

"Where do you think this dress shop is? What did Violet call it? Lovely's or something like that?" Daisy's head went from side to side, giving her the appearance of an addlebrained mule who couldn't decide which way to go. "Think it's on this side of the street, or that?"

She scanned the shops on both sides of Wylder Street and if she hadn't looked so ridiculous Lily would've let her continue to head bob.

"Lowery's. It's owned by a widow who Violet says can be a bit nosey, so watch what you say in the place. We don't want to be the talk of the town, do we?" Watching her sister's head sway from one side to the other began to make her dizzy so she added, "And stop that! You look ridiculous. The shop is near the mercantile so it's on this side of the street."

The other woman raised one eyebrow and glared. In the sunlight, her green eyes glittered like a cat's. "Hmmph. Interesting that you care so much what Wylder's gossips will say, given that you put on quite a show on the porch yesterday afternoon. Not a bit concerned then, were you?"

Leave it to the sisters to chatter behind her back.

"Violet shouldn't have told you anything. And what I do is my business—I'm the oldest, remember?" It would do them good to keep that in mind, that she deserved respect. "You two shouldn't talk about me behind my back."

"We didn't."

"Then how do you know what went on yesterday?"

They'd reached the dressmaker's shop. The stores in Charleston put this one to shame, they were so much bigger and grander, but looks might be deceiving. She certainly hoped so. If they couldn't get a decent dress in Wylder, where would they go?

Her sister paused on the steps leading to the dressmaker's front door. She sighed.

"I worried about you when you didn't arrive to Thomas' house. Violet said to stay with Lin and Alexia, but you're my sister, too. If something had happened to you, I wanted to be there to help." She paused, and the corners of her lips pulled up. "But from what I saw, you had all the help you needed, in the form of one very handsome fellow."

"Shh!" She looked behind them, but the lane stood empty. "I told you I don't want to start the gossip chain in this place. It's not like being at home, remember. People aren't as refined as those we're accustomed to."

"I'm sorry, then, for worrying about you." Her sister scowled, but even with a distasteful set to her lips and storm clouds in her green eyes, she still looked gorgeous. Daisy had been charmed since birth, and now, in this harsh place, she sparkled by comparison to the drabness surrounding them. "I won't do it again."

Before the other could stomp inside and cause a scene, Lily placed a hand on her arm to stop her.

"Wait. Thank you for your concern, I appreciate it." Her sister turned and met her gaze. There were still surges of a storm in the depths, but her eyes didn't shoot daggers, at least. "I'm really conscious of being an object of ridicule. I mean, after what happened with Warren…"

Daisy softened instantly. A gentle tone and a comforting hand placed upon hers. "That wasn't your fault."

"No, but people still talked. I heard the whispers and saw the sly looks. Believe me, I saw how amused people were to see me in such a low state." Thinking about it made her nauseated. She fought a wave of dizziness as she tried to smooth things over. "I didn't mean to come down so hard on you, I just want this to be a fresh start. I don't want to be embarrassed again, or gossiped about, or—oh, no."

She placed a hand over her mouth.

It couldn't be happening. Dear Lord, please—not

again! Maybe if she took a few deep breaths, she would gain control.

The other woman's eyes grew. "Lily? What's wrong?"

She couldn't speak.

When she most wanted to appear respectable and without reason to encourage gossip, her body betrayed her.

She dashed from the steps to the side of the building. She made it in time to duck her head out of view.

Hiding the retching noises proved impossible, but at least no one witnessed her losing her breakfast to the scrubby vegetation growing against the shop's side wall.

Chapter 20

Doctor Sullivan's piercing green eyes held Lily's gaze with such intensity that she squirmed under his scrutiny. He could see clear through to her soul, she knew he could. And, from the look on his face, he hesitated to state what he saw.

The man's shoulder length dark hair and beard sprinkled with gray made him appear kind, but she sensed steel beneath the friendly exterior. Being a doctor in these parts wouldn't do for anyone without an unbendable backbone or stomach impervious to the sights and smells he must witness. Her current ailment must seem tame to him, although a calamity for her.

Now, he stroked his beard with a thoughtful sigh.

Violet had insisted on sending for him and she felt so miserable that she'd agreed. Now, she wished she'd resisted.

Whatever came from this man's mouth would surely change her life.

Time to take the upper hand.

"I shouldn't have let my sisters ask you to come. It is, as you very well see, totally unnecessary." She smoothed down the front of her skirt with a firm hand. No fire burned in the hearth but the air in the parlor warmed her cheeks. Drawing a deep breath took effort, as well. The sooner she got the man to leave, the better. She needed to lie down. "I do thank you for coming and apologize for taking up your time."

A knock sounded on the door. It opened slowly and Violet poked her head in.

"Is there anything I can do to help?" She glanced from one face to the other, then looked at the doctor. "Will my sister recover? I am concerned, as you can imagine."

The man's southern charm put Lily at ease, even when her situation did not. It seemed he did the same for her sister, who joined them when he waved a hand for her to enter. She closed the door and crossed the room.

She did not appreciate being looked down on, so she patted the cushion beside her. When the other woman sat, the air seemed even warmer but hopefully it would only be for a moment. Surely, the doctor would take his leave soon.

"Sister, did the doctor tell you he's from the south, too? He served in the war, same as our father and brother did." She clasped her hands near her heart and glowed. "It is such a comfort to have a southern gentleman here in Wylder to look after us all."

It hit her that her sister and the doctor were cozy. How well did they know each other?

Time to throw the focus off her and onto another spot. "Tell me, have you been unwell since moving here?"

Violet shook her head. Her smile diminished a little. "No, of course not. Why do you ask?"

"It seems as if you and the doctor are well acquainted. I merely wondered if you've been ill, and perhaps reluctant to worry the family. You're sure you haven't kept something from us?"

She pulled her features into what she hoped showed worry. Hard to tell its effectiveness when the warmth suffocated her, and she dreamed of escaping the room.

"Nothing of the sort, I assure you." She shot the doctor a tiny smile. "Doctor Sullivan and I are acquaintances. This is a small town, you know. Everyone knows everyone, almost."

He returned the smile and ran a slow hand over his beard again. It seemed habitual, and she got the impression the man didn't realize he stroked the facial covering so often.

"Well, as we've known each other for nearly as long as you've been in town, I would hope we're friends by now, instead of merely acquaintances." He shrugged, and his broad shoulders stretched the fabric of the dark jacket he wore. "Actually, I think of you as family, if I'm not making you uncomfortable by sayin' that. I stood shoulder to shoulder with your kin in the stand against the north and in my book that makes us more than friends."

Violet reached out and placed her hand on the arm of the chair he occupied. Her eyes glistened and her voice came hardly above a whisper. "I feel the same, Coyote. You were one of the first people I met in town and you were so kind to me when I could barely remember my name. I will be forever grateful for that compassion."

Enough with the reminiscing! The man must leave—quickly, before all this sentiment turned her stomach over again and made her ill.

"So you were unwell when you arrived? Like my ailment, I imagine." She waved a dismissive hand. "I'm sure this will pass, the way it did for you. A matter of time, is all."

The doctor's eyebrows shot up. "I met your sister after she nearly froze to death in a snowbank several months after her arrival in Wylder. I admit, I should have attempted to make her acquaintance earlier but there are so many who require my care that sometimes it's hard to do so." He tugged on his beard and shook his head. "I'm getting sidetracked. But Violet did not show any signs of distress, other than being deep chilled and in need of rest when I first called on her."

"That's true, Lily. I did not have any stomach sickness, the way you do now. Not at all."

She took a deep breath. "Well, then I suppose it's a matter of time before I recover. Right, Doctor? Some rest and time will settle this?"

Now he inhaled deeply. He steepled his fingers, his elbows on the arms of the chair, and sat back. They looked at each other for what felt like an hour. Only a few heartbeats, she knew, but the man's penetrating gaze made her wriggle again. She did not like feeling like a worm on a hook.

"Miss Bloom, I suppose you might say that yes, it is a matter of time before this is taken care of." He glanced at her sister, then met her gaze again. "And I'm going to assume that you sisters are close enough for me to speak freely. There's really no way to hide the truth, anyhow. Violet will learn of your condition as the weeks pass."

Her sister grabbed her hand and held it in a death grip. "Oh, no! Whatever is wrong with Lily, we will find a way to cure her. I don't have much in the way of funds, but I can sell this house to pay for specialists.

What do we need to do? Coyote, help us, please!"

He leaned forward and put out a hand to stop her but when a schoolteacher gets a head of steam under her, it's near impossible to interrupt. Violet had been that way even as a child, so Lily shook her head and waved the doctor's hand away.

"You've got to let her run herself out." She twisted her hand from her sister's tight grasp. "You're hurting me. The doctor will have to treat me for broken fingers if you don't leave off."

"I didn't mean to do it." She turned her attention to the man sitting across from them. "What's wrong with her?"

He offered a kind smile. "Your sister is expecting a child. I'd say she's a couple of months along—and in perfect health. The sickness should leave off soon. It's perfectly normal for a woman to feel queasy when she's in the family way."

"Expecting!" The other woman's head whipped around so fast a hair pin went flying. "Lily—you're with child?"

The air in the room grew warmer. Now, a buzzing noise pushed its way into her head, as if a swarm of honeybees danced beside her ear.

She did not feel ill. In fact, for the first time since she'd journeyed westward, calmness swept over her. A welcome sensation given the turbulence of the past few months. She settled into the sticky, noisy ocean of serenity, sliding beneath its surface without a care.

And then, her eyes rolled up and she fell forward.

Chapter 21

Theo decided he must be bewitched. That had to be it.

It meant the woman with eyes so blue they'd make the Atlantic Ocean jealous must be a sorceress. What else could it be? How else could a woman bring feelings, emotions, and thoughts—good God, the thoughts she inspired!—like none he'd experienced before? She made him feel completely unlike himself.

She'd cast a spell on him. No other explanation he could imagine than that.

His stern mother would've grabbed him by the ear and hauled him off to church if she got wind of his thinking. Witches. Why, she didn't stand a hint of any such nonsense in her house. And while he'd left the red-brick home long ago, her influence crossed the miles between them.

Since he'd kissed Lily his lips twitched to kiss her again any time a thought of her passed through his mind. And since he couldn't get the woman out of his head, his mouth puckered and felt possessed—possessed by desire to kiss her again, that is.

He finally understood why men acted like such fools around women. He'd never been affected this way before but now that he had been it certainly explained a lot of things.

Thomas, for example. The man had gone from a

resolute no-women-allowed-in-my-life widower to someone who discussed meanings behind flowers, read poetry on porch swings, and ate whatever the woman who brought on these changes set before him. While his brother had been smitten with his wife before her passing, he'd never acted as addlepated as he did now.

Bewitched, too. Must be.

Theo closed his eyes and let the memory of holding Lily in his arms wash over him. The woman smelled like fresh-baked cookies and wildflowers all rolled in one. Her form fit against his as if they were puzzle pieces meant to be snugged together.

His mind roamed further, and he wondered just how well he'd fit into her…

Heat rose within him and it had nothing to do with the sun rising high in the sky. And rising…well, a certain part of him felt set to rise, too, so he opened his eyes and shook his head.

What the hell had gotten into him? His horse about to set foot on Wylder Street and here he sat, thinking about carnal relations with a woman he'd only met a short time ago.

Wei's Gemstones called to him. No one lingered near the humble shop and he enjoyed Wei's company, so he pulled up outside and tied his mare to the post.

Before he took two steps, the owner of the gemstone shop appeared in the doorway. Liu Wei came to the Territory from China. He'd been a doctor in his home country. Now he sold gemstones, created fancies like rings and earbobs for ladies, and dispensed traditional Chinese medicine when asked to do so.

An average-sized man, he dressed today in black trousers and gray button-down shirt. A bandanna wrapped around his neck. Despite the man's conventional dress, he presented a distinguished figure. Long black hair hung in a glistening braid down his back. And his eyes were so brown they were nearly black.

He raised a hand in greeting. "Good to see you, Wei. Are you busy?"

The other man shook his head. "Never too busy for a friend." He gestured to the door that stood open behind him. "Please, come inside. The sun has not found me in there yet."

The man's eloquent words were like music against the harsh conversation that dominated the western town. He brought an air of exotic mystery to the dusty streets.

Inside, a spotless room with a low wooden table against one wall where colorful gemstones spilled across its surface. There were a few pieces of jewelry, as well. Theo looked at each; they were pretty but didn't inspire him to reach for his wallet.

A pot-belly stove sat in one corner of the room with two straight-back wooden chairs nearby. In front of one chair, a table. Pliers and other small tools, along with an assortment of metal rings and stones, sat on top of it.

The proprietor held a hand toward one of the chairs. "Please, sit. I am happy to have company. It is a quiet afternoon in town."

Theo sat, placing his hat on a knee. He stretched his other leg out before him, finding comfort in the man's warm welcome.

"The sheriff would say to hold your tongue. We know how fast things can get lively around here." The truth, that Wylder could go from serene to shooting in a heartbeat, made him grin. "Quiet now. Loud later, maybe."

Wei tipped his head and chuckled. "True. So what has you thinking so deeply, my friend? I watched you ride down the street. Very clear that you have something of great importance on your mind."

Something of great importance.

Or someone.

Well, if that didn't cut straight to the heart of it.

He didn't bother to lie. He might be bewitched but he knew better than to insult a friend by giving a falsehood. "It's a woman."

The other gave a slow, thoughtful nod. "Ah, yes. Women do require a great deal of attention, don't they?"

"You have no idea."

A chuckle. "Oh, I assure you I do know how it feels. I confess, I, too, have a woman who haunts my thoughts. She is like a beautiful specter, here in my heart but not in my arms. Not yet, that is."

Wei and the woman who lived with the Bloom sisters, Sun Lin, were a couple. They'd been keeping company about as long as Violet and Thomas, but, like the other pair, did not seem ready to make a commitment.

"Yes, I guess you do." He pointed to the work on the table in front of Wei. "What are you making? Is that amber?"

The largest stone dangled from a gold chain. Along the length of the chain, smaller stones were set at intervals. One half looked complete but the other only had one side stone in place.

Wei picked the chain up. When he held it high, sunlight streaming through the window sent dazzling streaks of yellow across the space around them.

"You have a good eye. It is amber, from the northeastern region of China. I brought these with me when I came here and have been waiting for the perfect arrangement to come into my mind." He met Theo's gaze and smiled. "Today, the setting comes to me."

"It's beautiful." He pictured the necklace fastened around Lily's slender neck, with the largest bit of amber nestled against her skin near her breasts. His gut lurched, as if he stood on a rocking boat instead of firm land.

"Ah, I cannot take credit for that. The stones, they arrange themselves." Again the sunlight caught the center stone and sent fingers of gold across their faces. "Amber is a very special gemstone. It draws unease and pain from the physical, mental, and spiritual bodies. It gives the wearer a calm, happy disposition. Increased vitality is bestowed upon the wearer."

Increased vitality. He sure liked the way that sounded. And a happy disposition…he hadn't forgotten how prickly Lily had been when she stepped off the coach. If a woman could be ornery once, chances were good she might be that way again.

"Any way I can entice you to sell that amber necklace, Wei?"

Chapter 22

Lively dinner conversation did not make the night's menu. Lily hadn't expected it would so the stretches of silence did not surprise her.

The other women knew of her predicament. They'd heard her thud to the parlor floor and entered the room in time to see the doctor pick her up and carry her upstairs. She knew all of this from Violet, who sat by her side in that hard-seated, stiff-backed wooden chair in the bedroom where she woke.

Aside from inquiring about the bump on her forehead, her sisters made no mention of the doctor's declaration. That would not last. She knew *that* as surely as she knew her own name. They were mulling her situation over now but eventually the questions would begin. When they did, she'd be in it up to her ears.

Lily concentrated on savoring these last moments of peace. That they all didn't knock her over with questions and opinions offered some space to breathe.

Violet sighed, the sound so loud and long it could be heard in every corner of the modest kitchen.

"The schoolroom kept us busy this morning, didn't it, Lin?" She nodded to the woman sitting across the table from her.

"Oh, yes. Very busy." A poke at the potatoes on her plate with her fork, then, "Very much fun."

Her schoolteacher sister seemed determined to find some sense of normalcy. She pushed forward, even though her words sounded wooden. "We learned about the Great Wall, in China." When no one spoke, she went on. "It's my good fortune to have Lin here with us. She is knowledgeable about her home country and the children love hearing about it. Thank you for spending time in the schoolroom with me, Lin."

"My pleasure to talk about China."

"It's the ideal way to bring a geography lesson to life." Her sister gave her a small smile before she stabbed a green bean and ate it. "I could never get those children to have any idea what China is like without Lin's help. And there are two Chinese children in town now. They don't attend the school—yet—but I'm hopeful it will happen."

"Yes, I spoke with the mother this afternoon." The Chinese woman nodded, sending the thick, glistening black braid she wore sliding along one shoulder of her dress. "She wants the children to learn but we are working on their English."

Violet sounded relieved. "I'm glad to hear that. I hate to think of children in town not getting an education. I mean, that's what I'm here for." She put her fork down and snapped her fingers. "Will it help if I send over some McGuffey Readers? They worked well enough to help you with your language skills. Maybe the children will find them useful, too."

Lin nodded. "Yes, they were helpful. I would not speak this well if not for you and McGuffey."

Daisy dropped her fork on the edge of her plate with a clatter that silenced both women.

"Look, I think it's wonderful that Lin is here, and I

would love to hear about China, too, when there's time. But tonight? It does not seem like the moment to discuss children or the school—or even China!" She paused and met Lin's startled gaze. "I apologize. That probably sounds awful and I mean no disrespect."

A tip of the chin from the woman whose birthplace came under discussion showed she was not offended by the outburst.

Their hostess put her fork down, as well. She glanced at to her right, where the subject of their discussion sat.

Lily felt every gaze in the place on her. Six eyes, all inquisitive and boring a hole into her face. She considered not looking up, not meeting their gazes or giving the answers they ached to hear.

Hightailing it out of Wylder crossed her mind. She could hop the Union Pacific out of town, head to Cheyenne or Laramie where no one knew her and fade into obscurity. It would work.

If she were destined for obscurity, which she most certainly was not!

No, she'd leave running away for the faint of heart.

She placed her fork on the edge of her plate, wiped her hands across the napkin on her lap, and inhaled. Then she looked up and, as she suspected, found three pairs of probing eyes turned on her.

"What?" She spread her hands wide. "What do you want me to say?"

Daisy quirked a brow. It irked her that in the moment her younger sister wore a smug expression. "I'd think the question is more of a 'who?' than a 'what?' if you want me to be honest about what I'm thinking."

Violet cleared her throat. Color rose on her cheeks. "I'm wondering 'when?'—as in, were you…ah, when you left Charleston, were you, ah, I mean—"

"Pregnant!" Daisy slapped her hand down on the table with enough force the water in their glasses swayed. "The word is pregnant, sister—and you shouldn't be embarrassed to say it, either. Goodness, women have been getting pregnant since…well, since forever. And now our dear, eldest, most revered sister is the one who's got herself knocked up."

Lily's fingers clenched. Smacking the sarcasm right out of her sister would turn this conversation around, but it would surely get her tossed out of the house, as well. These sisters weren't much but right now they were all she had. She struggled to remain calm.

The Chinese woman had been quiet but at Daisy's latest eruption she dropped her fork and covered her mouth with a hand. Her eyes, so round and beautifully dark, grew so large that they looked ready to pop from her head.

Their hostess reacted exactly as one would expect a schoolteacher to—she snapped her fingers, raised a hand to stop the conversation, and shot each sister a glare. The color rose higher in her cheeks, but anger chased embarrassment.

"Stop it." She hitched a breath and turned her attention on the wide-eyed woman. "I'm so sorry, Lin. My sisters are acting like common street urchins and showing our family in a poor light. Please, excuse their rude behavior."

Lin gave a nod. "No need to apologize." She picked up her plate and began to stand. "I leave you sisters to talk."

A hand wave from their hostess dropped her back into the chair. "Don't leave. You're family, too—you're as much a sister to me as anyone else in this room, so stay, please."

The uproar bought Lily time, but she had no idea what to say, really. What more could they want? The fact sang clear: She had a difficult situation and had no idea how to cope.

The silver lining, that the sickness should abate soon. The doctor seemed certain it would only be a week or so longer before she stopped vomiting. That lightened her spirits more than anything had in the past months. If only she could chuck the rest of what weighed on her shoulders.

That had been a thought since she'd heard the doctor's pronouncement, that she should divest herself of the situation entirely. But how? And, more importantly, did she have the stomach for such a thing?

She didn't think she did, although the idea of walking away from this sounded almost too good to resist.

The almost. That's what caught her.

Violet spoke in a gentler tone. "Lily, we are your family. We care for you and want to help, but we can't do that if we're kept in the dark. Now, would you please let us in on what's happened?"

She shrugged. "I suppose I have no choice, do I?"

Her sister ignored that and went on. "Did the doctor's diagnosis come as a surprise to you?"

"I suspected as much." She sighed. "But I hoped to be wrong."

Silence fell over the room. She leaned into it,

loving the way they all shut up and stopped snapping at her. Being the center of this showed how a rabbit on the run from wolves must feel.

The respite didn't last long.

Daisy drummed her fingertips on the tabletop. Honestly, the girl acted like she'd been brought up in a stable.

"Stop it, will you?" She placed a hand against her brow. "That incessant noise will make me feel unwell again, and that is the last thing I need. Besides, how do you ever hope to get a husband with ink-stained, calloused fingers? Really, sister, consider yourself."

Despite her condition, it fell to her to lead the sisterhood. They'd best remember that.

The drumming ceased, but a shriek of laughter replaced it. When it ripped through her mind her fingers clenched again.

"Consider myself? Isn't that the kettle calling the pot black?" Daisy stood, grabbed her plate, and crossed to the sink. She slipped it into the dish pan before turning back and leaning a hip against the wooden counter. "Have you forgotten how I held your shoulders while you were sick earlier today? Or how I've endured your snippy remarks as we crossed the country? And maybe it's slipped your mind that I'm the one who left her life and journeyed out here with you—you, whose life blew apart in Charleston. I could have let you come west alone, the way Violet did, but I came with you. That, dear sister, is something *you* ought to consider."

Chapter 23

No one tried to stop Lily when she left the dinner table to go to bed early.

The looks of relief clearly showed on their faces—and matched the feeling she carried with her. The energy it took to explain what happened had long left her. Best for everyone for the discussion to drop while she took her leave.

A decent night's sleep, that's what they all needed. She'd fallen under the Sandman's spell the moment her head touched the pillow and had slept the entire night through.

Sunshine crept through the divide in the white curtain panels and brushed her cheek. Warm, comforting, and bright, it offered a coziness that she so desperately needed. She basked in the light, holding the glow as close to her heart as possible. It might be the last peaceful moment she had, and she knew it.

She opened one eye and peeked at the other bed. Empty.

So, the trio had already convened. Surely she occupied the central place in their gossipy discussions.

How had her life fallen this low? She should be planning her wedding, not hiding in a tiny bedroom in the middle of nowhere wondering how she'd survive what lay before her.

But survive it, she must. And late in the night,

she'd decided that the babe would remain, as well. Disgust that she'd even considered not keeping it washed over her, even as she made excuses to herself about it being better off with a family than a single mother. She brushed it all aside. The day would prove difficult enough—no need to scold herself.

She slid from bed and got herself ready to face what could not be avoided. Her morning routine suffered but she made it downstairs in short order, expecting to find the women assembled and waiting.

Every room sat empty. Tidy, homey—and completely without human occupants.

A wave of uncertainty hit her. Should she look for them?

She found a note on the entry table. They'd all gone to the schoolhouse, and they welcomed her joining them if she wanted.

Well, she didn't want.

A reprieve from their probing eyes could not be squandered. She grabbed her reticule and headed for the front door. Time to explore Wylder on her own.

She stepped out onto the porch and pulled the door closed behind her.

"Well, exactly the person I hoped to see." Theo stood beside a wagon stopped beyond the picket fence. In casual dress, he looked almost handsomer than he had in his Sunday best. Something about a man wearing low-slung blue denim pants, boots, and a blue chambray shirt screamed rugged. Add the Stetson he held loosely in one hand and the reins in the other, and her senses were heightened even more. "It must be my lucky day. And you, looking pretty as a June bug on a daffodil."

Lily walked down the gravel path, past the blooming flowers, smiling. They were pretty but the man's words made her feel as if she out-bloomed them all.

"And here I thought you weren't one for that 'romance' stuff."

He feigned surprise, placing a hand over his heart and taking a tiny step backward. "Why, wherever did you get such a notion?"

"From you, just yesterday."

With a chuckle, he shrugged. "I daresay you've got a good memory."

His lips turned up when he smiled, and when they did that her heart flopped around like a fish on the seashore. A sensation both fabulous and disconcerting, all at once.

"Not always."

He raised one eyebrow. "Now that makes me nervous."

She shook her head and tugged on the strings of her reticule before she remembered how unflattering it looked for a woman to fiddle with anything. Her hands went to her sides as she met his gaze.

"No need to be nervous. I only mean that I recall what's important to me. The rest I forget as quickly as I can." She didn't want to appear shallow, so she added, "I mean, why cloud a mind with meaningless details? Keep the essentials and let the rest blow away."

Theo ran a hand down the neck of the sleek animal that nudged his shoulder. "You are a wise woman, Lily Bloom. Very wise, indeed."

The praise made something in her belly jump. At least she hoped that's what did it. She wasn't mentally prepared to feel the baby move. Not yet. And if the flutter were a prelude to another bout of queasiness... She shook the thought from her head. Best to not even entertain that idea.

Time to change the subject, before he said anything else that either heated her up or made her insides quiver. Both of those reactions were too risky. The last thing she wanted to do—well, better to reduce the chance she'd embarrass herself.

"To what do I owe this pleasant surprise? I certainly didn't expect to find you here when I came outside."

He tapped his hat against his thigh and scraped the toe of a boot across the dirt. In that instant he looked like a mischievous schoolboy.

"Well, it's like this: I kinda hoped I'd run into you, so I moseyed into town to see if I'd spot you out and about."

She grinned. "So you weren't sitting outside Violet's house waiting for me to emerge?"

"Nope. I actually just drove up and figured I'd knock on the door." He tapped his hat again and shrugged. "I already drove down most of Wylder's streets, hoping to see you. When I didn't, I thought you might still be at home."

"You figured right." She drew in a deep breath. "Well, now that you've found me, what next?"

"I hoped you might agree to come for a ride with me. A longish one, out of town."

Her curiosity sent a tingle along her nerve endings. "Longish? Like to California?"

When he chuckled again her body warmed. The sound, so deep and masculine, filled her with a desire to hear it more often. As in, all the time.

"Not that long." He met her gaze and lingered a moment, letting their eyes speak without words. "No, I kind of hoped you'd agree to come out to the homestead for a bit. I'd like to show you that there's more to Wylder than what you see here in town."

Chapter 24

The wagon ride to Theo's land proved Lily's theory that the stagecoach route had been littered with the bones of the dead, a path to the devil's playground that no one should travel. When they set out she feared this journey would be the same, but she should have known better.

The man beside her hummed a pleasant tune, turned to smile at her every few minutes, and handled the reins with a gentle touch. He certainly did not seem the type to drag a woman across bumpy miles of hard road.

The landscape out of town proved a surprise. She'd imagined endless dusty acres dotted with withered, dead vegetation. As with the stagecoach route, lots of grave markers and discarded bits of broken wagons. She scanned the plains, but she saw none of that.

Endless plains stretched toward the horizon. To the north, a ribbon of railroad track with a mountain range in the distance. She supposed it must be the one she'd admired from the bench on Sunday, before the chicken flew at her. The hills had been pretty from town but were even more captivating now, with nothing to distract from their magnificence.

Theo stopped humming. "Pretty, isn't it?"

She nodded. "It certainly is. Honestly, this isn't what I expected." Turning to face him, she raised her shoulders, then let them fall. "After the ghastly trip out, I thought this would be a continuation of that desolation. But it's nothing like that, and I'm glad."

His smile sent her heart tripping in her chest. It took so little to please the man.

"Well, I'm glad to hear it. And I believe you'll be even more surprised when you see where I'm taking you."

"Is it far?" She wondered if she should've left a note for her sisters. What if they worried?

Well, maybe it'd do them some good to worry about her. Neither had been very compassionate about her situation last night and it still peeved her. Yes, they could fret a bit.

"Nope. I'm fortunate, the claim is nearer to town than many others. It makes it easy to come in for supplies and such." He turned to her and winked. "Also a good thing for courting purposes."

Heat flooded her cheeks. The man's charm, a burst of cool air after a long, hot stretch, nourished her. It had been too long since a man showed kindness. She'd missed it more than she realized.

"Ah, yes, that would be an advantage." She lifted her cheeks toward the sound of birdsong before swinging her head around to meet his gaze. "Tell me, are you courting anyone special?"

The passed a stand of scrub pines. The wagon wheels quieted when they rumbled over fallen pine needles. The debris sent a sweet scent into the air. They rode through the pine cloud without speaking.

"I'd say I'm calling on a very special lady. One of unrivaled beauty and refinement. A lady who travels across endless miles, arrives in a distant land, and settles in so swiftly that I can't remember a day when she didn't live here." He paused, then shot her a fast grin. "And she cleans up real well, too."

She let the words sink in for a long moment. Theo had returned to humming and didn't seem to expect a reply, so she didn't scramble to come up with one. How different to speak with a man who didn't wait for her to twitter and gasp over his every proclamation. A nice change of pace, this western cowboy.

But he'd come out west, too. He hadn't been born here, yet he fit in so well.

"You're from back east, aren't you?" The question tumbled from her mouth. It didn't flow with their conversation but that couldn't be helped. "You weren't born in the territory, were you?"

They'd reached a river, so he turned the wagon toward the trail that ran along its banks. The air here, soft, cool, and fresh, swept over them when he slowed the horse to a leisurely walk.

"I hail from Pennsylvania. Moved out here a few years after Thomas and his wife." He nodded toward the mountains that were now in front of them, a stunning vista she could barely take her gaze from. "Lived in town, planned to stake my own claim…then, the unthinkable happened."

Alexia hinted that her mother did not reside with her and Thomas, but she hadn't said precisely why that was the case.

She turned to the man beside her. His presence, so strong and rugged, made her feel safe. She'd heard of attacks on innocent travelers and had worried about being accosted on a lonely trail, but his confidence chased those fears away. "What happened?"

Theo quirked a brow and glanced over at her. "You mean your sister hasn't told you?"

She shook her head. "Violet and I aren't that close. I mean, I am older than she is and, well, you know how that is."

"I'm surprised. She always speaks so highly of her sisters. I thought you were all thick as thieves." He softened the last bit with a small smile. "To answer your question, Thomas' wife died. In childbirth. That's why he vacated his homestead. All that hard work, so much time and money, sweat and even blood put into the place, yet he couldn't stand to remain without her."

"He must have loved her very much to walk away from the life they built."

He spoke softly. "I've never seen a couple more devoted than they were."

They rode in silence for a few minutes.

Deserted prairie had given way to a more inviting view. Bursts of green foliage dotted the shadows beyond the trail. Ponderosa pines scented the air. Clumps of wildflowers spilled from crevasses between rocky outcroppings. Moss clung to rocks at the edge of the river.

"That must have been so sad, losing someone like that."

He nodded. "For everyone. Alexia suffered greatly. She'd been waiting on being the big sister to the new baby for months. It never occurred to any of us that the birth would take such a bad turn." He looked over at her and she saw sadness lingered in his eyes. "No one wants to lose a baby, or a wife, for that matter—and Thomas lost both in one heartbeat. How could he stay out here after that?"

A change of subject seemed in order, so she waited a few moments, then asked, "How much longer before we reach your place?"

He grinned. "We've been on my land for a while now." He tipped his head toward a rise ahead. "See that? Right on the other side is the house. A fine view of the river, tucked into the slope of a small hill, nice stand of trees beside it. Wish I'd been the one to choose the site, or the claim. Thomas did real well with it all and I'm grateful he sold it to me but still, a man wants to stake his own claim, doesn't he?"

The horse moved faster now. As they crested the rise in the road, the homestead came into view. She hadn't known what to expect. Sod houses and tiny cabins were spoken about so she thought Theo might own something like that.

But a solid wood-frame structure, complete with porch and a second story, came into view. She spotted a fenced garden, a couple of outbuildings, and a good-sized barn.

"Son of a bitch!" Theo urged the horse to move faster.

"What's wrong?" She grabbed the side of the wooden seat to keep from being jostled out of the wagon. She scanned the property but saw nothing concerning. Certainly no reason for the man to swear. "Why are you barreling to the house as if the devil is on our tail?"

He jutted his chin toward three riders. They were headed toward the house and by the set of Theo's jaw he knew who they were.

"I'd rather have Old Scratch himself on my property than that bunch."

Chapter 25

Lily went to the porch as Theo instructed but she stood close enough to hear the exchange. If she'd believed the man simply a charming, unmarried homesteader she underestimated him.

The man who stood beside his wagon waiting on the riders to draw up looked formidable. He'd pushed his jacket back to reveal the twin pistols he wore low on each hip. In his hands, a rifle pulled from beneath the wagon seat.

Three men rode into the space. Two wore dusty hats and boots, were rangy with craggy, sun-bronzed faces. The third, in a black jacket and boots that looked new even to her unpracticed eye, grimaced when his horse took the command to stop abruptly.

Theo's hat brim sent a swath of shade that hid his features, but his voice left no room for interpretation.

"You're on private property."

The closest man pushed his hat back on his head, crossed his wrists over the saddle's pommel, and leaned forward. The nonchalant air purely an affectation, as the other dusty man's hands went to his gun belt and his gaze raked the area beyond the house.

"Now, you know we're just passin' through." The man spat a stream of tobacco juice at the ground beside his horse. "We been through this a'fore, Harvey."

"We have. I've told you to stay off my land."

The man in the shiny boots spoke. He had a high, squeaky voice and waved his hands to punctuate his words. "We didn't mean any harm. These gentlemen were showing me some property the other side of yours. I'm thinking of staking a claim. Trying to find the best fit for me and my family, that's all."

Theo waved the rifle barrel. "Well, mister, you'd best forget 'bout puttin' in a claim on any property that borders mine."

"Why is that?" The man's twang gave him away. He had to be from somewhere back east. Boston would be her guess. He sounded as if he had a fish up his nose and now his voice shook. "It looks like a fine parcel."

They might be on horseback, but Theo didn't seem bothered by it. His glare could have melted mountains.

The silent man shot him a look of disgust.

His partner, the one who spoke first, spat again.

The newcomer urged his horse to take a step backward.

"Forget whatever they showed you. First off, they're not gentlemen. They're looking to rob your pockets with their fee for showing you about and filin' your claim. You don't need them—you can file your own damn claim."

The copious spitter snarled. "That's a lie. We ain't tryin' to rob nobody. We're honest businessmen, and you know that, Harvey!"

"What I know is that you've been told to steer clear of here, to stay off my land, and to stop showin' people any land borderin' mine." He looked from one man to the other, ignoring the one whose desire to stake a claim brought them here. "Now get your sorry asses off my land—and don't come back!"

"You can't talk to us that way—" The nasally tone increased when the newcomer became indignant.

Theo's hands moved so fast they were a blur, but she heard a cartridge slide into the rifle's chamber. He raised it to his shoulder and pointed it at the blustering man.

"My Winchester says I can talk however I damn well please. Now, turn your sorry asses around and get off my land before I have to blow a hole in one of you." He paused, moving the rifle a hair to the left, toward the silent one whose hand rested near the pistol on his right hip. "And I don't care who I hit first."

The spitting man spat one more time. "C'mon, let's get outta here." They turned their horses around, but he looked back over his shoulder before he rode off. "Land around here ain't all that great after all."

Lily's heart thudded in her chest and it had nothing at all to do with being enchanted with the man standing in the yard, although she did feel even more in awe of him than she had earlier. Watching him chase three armed men off like that surely gave his already ruggedly handsome character a boost.

But that didn't make her heartbeat feel like a stallion galloped inside her.

She exhaled the breath she didn't realize she held and placed a hand over her chest. Fear did funny things to a woman, including making her head feel woozy.

"Oh, my…" Her eyes fluttered and her knees wobbled.

Theo rushed across the yard and took the steps in one long stride. He leaned the weapon against the railing and gathered her in his arms, holding her tightly against his chest.

A mix of spice, horse, and a wonderfully masculine mix of starched cotton and sweat swept up her nose. She inhaled deeply, filling the spaces claimed by fear with the essence of his calm strength.

"I'm so sorry—I should've sent you inside." He opened the front door and carried her into the parlor and went directly to an overstuffed chair beside the fireplace. The hearth sat cold, but sunlight heated the room well enough. He laid her gently on the dark blue cushion, then raised her feet and placed them on a matching ottoman. "There. Relax while I grab you a drink."

She raised a hand to stop him, but he left the room without looking back.

She surveyed her surroundings. A large room, with an ornately carved mantel above the fireplace. Built-in bookshelves on the far wall. It did not look like a bachelor's lodgings—and it most certainly did not resemble a sod home or cabin.

No, the comfortable air about the place conveyed the love that had gone into its construction. The original owners had left but their love lingered.

He returned with two glasses. He handed her one and watched while she took a sip.

Lemonade. Her favorite.

"Why, that tastes like home." She took a second sip and felt the fuzziness leave her head. "It surely does make me feel as if I'm back home in Charleston, in Mother's drawing room. Thank you, Theo."

Her feet did not take up the full space on the ottoman, so he sat beside them.

"I'm glad you like it. So, feeling better? You went white as a cloud out there."

She nodded. "I'm fine. Overcome by the excitement, I guess. Sorry to be such a bother."

"You're no bother. I'm the one who's sorry. I never should have let you witness such vulgar behavior." He swirled the liquid in his glass before he took another drink. "I shudder to think what opinion you have of me now that you've seen that I'm not as gentlemanly as you might have believed. I hate that I've been diminished in your eyes."

His gaze when it met hers underscored his words. She believed him, that he felt unhappy at possibly losing her high regard. No man had ever cared what she thought of him, not really. The southern bluster she'd grown up with showed itself now in its whole truth: a smokescreen designed to convey sentiments that were either entirely false or only marginally true.

He stared at her with sorrow in his deep brown eyes. Clearly, what happened since their arrival did not match his plan for the day.

"You need not worry. If anything, you've grown even more…" Heat swept across her chest, and she hoped her neck wasn't turning pink.

"Even more what?"

She'd painted herself into a corner.

"Remember, we've got a pact to tell each other the truth." His tone was gentle, but his words were serious. "Even if the sentiment isn't flattering, don't hide it, please."

She raised her gaze from the glass in her hand. "Oh, no, there's nothing unflattering about what I'm thinking. You were magnificent out there. I don't understand why those men were on your property, not entirely, but I think it's so brave of you to chase them off the way you did."

He raised one eyebrow and surveyed her with a tiny grin on his face. A lock of hair fell across his brow. She would've loved the chance to push it back into place but that would involve leaning forward—and she felt sure that if she did that she'd lean right into his arms and stay there.

"Well, you're surely a surprise, Lily. You arrive so starched and prim, almost downright prissy, and yet here you are, making allowances for the man you believed must be the town drunk." He chuckled. "An unlikely turn of events, don't you think?"

She scowled at him, but purely for effect. The tone in his voice tugged at her heartstrings. No other dared to tease her this way. "Are you complaining?"

He shook his head and bent forward. "Not one bit."

They were close enough that she felt his warm breath on her lips.

Close enough that the scent of him, so strong and alluring, swept up her nose.

So near that all either of them had to do…

She tilted her head and ended the distance between them. Theo's lips met hers with an eagerness that matched the enthusiasm in her own heart. When they kissed the whole world fell away.

Everything, except the man who pulled her into his arms and onto his lap, ceased to exist—including the child growing within her.

Chapter 26

"Well, look who showed up, finally." Violet stood when Lily walked into the front parlor. She clasped her hands at her waist, showing the full side of her schoolteacher ways, and wrinkled her forehead disapprovingly. "We were nearly tempted to send out a search party for you, sister."

That her younger sister scolded her at all, let alone before a roomful of people, should have set her teeth on edge but she smiled and ran a hand across her hair. Not a hairpin out of place, the way she liked.

"Oh, don't be so dramatic. Surely you knew I'd be with Theo."

He came into the room and stood beside her. He'd dropped his Stetson on the table inside the door and now ran his fingers through his thick, dark hair.

"We didn't mean to worry you." He nodded to Daisy, Lin, Alexia, and Thomas. Then he turned his broad smile on Violet. "It's my fault that Lily didn't let anyone know where she went. I sort of scooped her up from the porch this morning and took her on an adventure. So, you see, she didn't mean to be out so long—it's all on me. Forgive me?"

The look on the man's face could've charmed the pants off Saint Peter.

Her sister turned pink when he met her gaze and winked. "It won't happen again, I promise."

"Well, then, how can I stay out of sorts?" She smiled at him, then glanced at Lily. "I worried about you, is all. You're our sister and you're not accustomed to life in the west. We aren't in Charleston anymore, you know."

Lily crossed the room and sat on the settee beside Alexia. The young girl moved over enough that she had extra room for another person, if they chose to sit. Which she, of course, hoped would happen.

Now that Theo no longer sat beside her in the buggy, she missed the feel of his shoulder rubbing against hers, the security of his strong, warm body nearby, and the way he made her tummy flutter when he spoke. The ride back to Wylder had been much too short and she would have lingered longer in his home, but he'd insisted they be back before dinner.

So here they were.

And she missed him, even though he hadn't yet left.

"I'm perfectly aware this isn't the place where we grew up, Violet. I'm sorry that I worried you, but you needn't have wasted the effort. I'm fine, as you can see."

Daisy grinned from across the room. She held her open notebook on her lap, but the pages did not capture her attention. "Yes, we see you are looking very fine, sister. Almost giddy, even."

Leave it to the writer to add a dimension to a description. For once, she wished her sister were occupied with her messy ink and endless scribbles.

Alexia turned to her and asked, "Giddy?"

"My sister is being silly. Pay no attention to her." She scrambled to change the subject. "What are you all doing, anyhow? Looks like a meeting in here, one we weren't invited to."

"We, indeed…" A finger traced the outer pages of the book and Lily knew that had her sister a pen nearby and she'd take notes on this conversation.

The child came to her rescue. "Daisy is reading to us. She writes stories, you know, and they are mighty interesting. Maybe I'll be a writer when I grow up, too." She stretched out her hands on her lap and examined her fingers. "Only I'm not keen on penmanship, am I, Miss Bloom?"

Violet crossed the room and sat in a chair beside Thomas, who perched on the edge of the wide stone hearth. She smiled at the girl. "You do well enough, when you keep your mind on the task at hand."

Daisy looked thoughtful. "I heard tell of a machine that makes letters on paper—before we left Charleston, that is. I don't remember what it's called but if that's really a thing I believe I'll need to get one." She smiled at Alexia. "And of course if I do you'll be welcome to use it, too."

A fast clap of the hands accompanied a little hop on the seat. The movement made Lily's belly lurch but not as badly as she knew it could.

Theo sat down beside her, and she instantly forgot about her tummy. His presence calmed her.

"Are you going to keep reading, Daisy?" Thomas placed his hand on the arm of Violet's chair. Close enough to be cozy but not improper. Apparently they were keeping up appearances, even after such a long courtship and despite the wilderness surrounding them.

"I think not. We ended at a good point to begin again." She closed the book, then looked around the room. "Is it just me, or are the rest of you ready for dinner, too?"

"Good thought. It's a fine time to gather for dinner. We have an easy meal today, so it won't take but a minute to get it on the table." Violet agreed as soon as Daisy made the suggestion.

Her sisters and Lin rose and headed for the kitchen. Alexia did, too, hurrying eagerly with the others to help.

Thomas nodded to Lily before she could rise.

"So, did Theo take you out to the homestead?"

Memories of their time together brought a flush to her cheeks. She raised a hand to her face and smiled. "He did. What a lovely ride."

"It sure is beautiful at this time of year. Perfect drive, for sure." He smiled. "So, did you like the place?"

The intensity in his eyes showed that it mattered what she thought. She remembered he'd built the homestead for his own family, before their world turned upside down. Every inch must still hold a piece of his heart.

She answered without hesitation. "I did. It's such a gorgeous piece of land and the house is utterly captivating. The gardens are beginning to show signs of blooming and, honestly, what's not to love? It is wonderful."

Theo placed a hand over hers for an instant. The fleeting touch sent her heart skittering in her chest. "I'm so glad you feel that way, especially after the unpleasantness."

His brother narrowed his eyes. "What unpleasantness?"

"Those two were back, with a newcomer from back east, showing him the land adjacent to mine."

"Didn't you run them off?" Thomas scowled. "More than once, even?"

Theo nodded. "I have."

"They're not taking the hint to stay away? You know, you might need to show 'em the place really is off limits."

She looked from one brother to the other. Something passed between them, unspoken, but tangible. She wondered if she read them correctly. There seemed only one way to stop the men from trespassing, and they were in the west—and lawlessness supposedly abounded.

Her throat tightened.

Theo must be planning to shoot the men. What else could it be?

Chapter 27

Theo looked over his shoulder.

He thought he'd been followed but nothing out of the ordinary lay behind him on Wylder Street. The usual assortment of riders on horseback, miners dragging heavily burdened mules in their wake, women out for necessities, a few from neighboring tribes come to town to trade their goods, ranch hands with time off… Nothing to raise his internal danger alarm. Still, he'd been sure someone tailed him.

The door to Addison's law office stood open so he stepped inside. Red dust from the street beyond covered the first few feet of wooden flooring, the fine coat a reminder that it hadn't rained in far too long. The western frontier parched beneath the unrelenting sun and despite efforts to keep the outdoors where it belonged, it invaded.

Addison looked up from the stack of papers on his desk. He stood, held out a hand, and when they'd shaken he gestured to a chair. "You look near fried. Take a load off."

He placed his hat on one knee, took the bandanna from his jacket pocket, and mopped his face and neck. "I feel fried, believe me. When I think it can't get any hotter, it does." He kicked a toe in the dust at his feet. "And I bet that when you think you've got all the dust Wylder has to offer more comes in."

The other man shook his head. "I don't know how the hell it blows in. God knows, there ain't a breeze to be found between here and the Pacific."

"Truer words were never spoken. We need a good gully-washer to break this heat."

"We do." The attorney shuffled his papers into a pile and tossed them into a drawer. He closed it with the butt of one hand, then threaded his fingers together on his desk. "Not that I mind jawin' about the weather with you but I'm pretty sure that's not what brought you in here. What's up?"

Theo hated to bring his troubles to anyone, but he needed advice—the kind that would quench his concerns about being the guest of honor at a necktie social if he found himself in the position to pull a trigger.

"A while back I mentioned those no-goods who won't stay off the homestead. Do you remember?"

A nod. "I do. Don't tell me they've come back again."

"They did. And draggin' some poor guy who don't know 'em for who they really are. Chased 'em off again, but I expect they'll not stay chased for too long."

The attorney shook his head. He huffed a breath, steepled his fingers, and wrinkled his brow. Theo gave him a minute to consider, being he had come for the man's advice.

Addison spread his hands wide. "Damn shame. They're gonna force you to do something you probably don't want to do. If they'd leave without a fuss and stay away they'd save themselves a whole lotta trouble." He ran a hand through his hair. "But some fools just won't see the truth even when it's biting them on the nose."

"What if I've got to do more than bite 'em? What if I'm pushed into that corner, Addison? How hard will it be to prove I had a right to do what I did?"

Theo hadn't considered any of this before meeting Lily but now that he thought about bringing a woman to the homestead he had to be clear on his rights. If he crossed a line he had to be sure it wouldn't affect a wife and family to the extent that they'd be without recourse. He couldn't jeopardize the home and all he'd worked for.

But he wouldn't put up with trespassers, either.

"A man's got a right to defend what's his. If you're pushed, you do what you've got to do. Trust me, I haven't lost a case yet where a homeowner defended his property." A knowing smile broke out on the attorney's face. "Does this have anything to do with you bringing a wife into the picture? I've never heard you concerned about self-defense before, but a man's ideas change when there's a woman involved."

Relief that he needn't bother about whatever he had to do to protect his home shot through him. He offered a smile, too. "Yeah, it has all to do with that. I mean, I can't be worrying I can't protect my home and family without maybe leaving the woman in the lurch. I've seen women without men, and it's not a pretty sight, watching them struggle. I won't have that for a woman I bring to the homestead."

He stood. Taking up more time of the man's than necessary wasn't something he would do. "Thanks for your advice. I'll rest easier now that I've talked with you."

"Anytime I can help, I'm here."

They shook again, then Theo put his hat onto his

head and turned toward the door. When Addison cleared his throat, he turned back to face him.

"One last thing, Theo. When you take a wife and bring her to the homestead, be sure you teach her how to use a rifle. There's no guarantee you'll be home when someone trespasses or tries to make trouble, so be sure your woman is a good shot."

"Thanks. I'll do that."

The other man nodded and gave a smile. "And rest assured, I'm just as good at proving women need to defend their property as men do. If it comes to it, I'll take care of her. You just make sure she can hit what she's aimin' at."

Chapter 28

It occurred to Lily that life in the small lavender house settled into a routine. It happened quickly, without fanfare, and seemingly with no effort on anyone's part.

During the week Violet left for the schoolhouse early, often with Lin at her side. Sometimes the quiet Chinese woman returned home midday to flit about the place like a lovely butterfly. She kept order and cooked most meals. She added beauty with wildflowers that spilled from Mason jars in every room.

Daisy did what she did best: She read a lot and wrote even more. The western air seemed to agree with her. Her cheeks filled out, most days she leapt from bed before dawn to sit on the back porch and watch the sunrise, and she and Lin had begun to teach Alexia how to bake. All in all, she appeared happy.

Both of her sisters did. And that sat well with her.

Normally it would have annoyed her that they were so serene and somewhat settled while her own course in life had been thrown so off-kilter, but she found it mattered less than it might have. Perhaps the dry Wylder air worked its magic on her, too. Who could tell?

Thankfully the queasiness had all but ended. That blessing almost gave the illusion that she could not be, as Daisy so boldly put it, knocked up.

They'd all left off trying to discuss it with her after she'd refused their attempts to open that conversation. After a couple of tries, they stopped, which gave her breathing room. She still had no idea what to do but at least she didn't feel chased by a pack of inquisitive hounds.

Sunshine made the front porch glow. She stepped out, adjusted her hat, and paused.

It hit her that she didn't have obligations to anyone save herself.

Her social calendar had never been this clear. In Charleston there were parties to attend and visits to make. More to host and plan. Charity work to attend to and the household affairs she helped Mother oversee.

Now, she had nothing. And it felt entirely liberating.

"Off to town?" Daisy sprawled in a chair at the far end of the porch. An open volume of Shakespeare lay face down on her lap. "Great day for a stroll, isn't it?"

She didn't have a destination in mind, only thought to get out and take some air. But her sister had a point, the day called to those with a wandering disposition.

Now she looked at her sister. They had been getting on better the past few days, and it made her more inclined to spend time with the family author. A parcel waited posting upstairs and since she did have a letter to send home to Mother…

"Perfect day for a walk. I'm headed to the post office. Would you like to come along?"

As she expected would happen, the other woman closed the book with a fast snap and jumped to her feet. "Yes, I would love that! Violet says it is over by the stagecoach office so it's not far at all." She dashed to the door and opened it. "Wait right here, I'll be back in a second. I have to dash upstairs for a parcel and my hat."

"Take your time. You don't need to rush. I'm not leaving without you." To prove the point, she sat on the edge of the small wooden bench beside the door and folded her hands on her lap. "I'll be here when you're ready."

Daisy pulled her brows together, giving her a puzzled look, before she nodded and went inside.

She couldn't blame her sister for being surprised by her relaxed attitude. The truth, that the eldest couldn't afford to be complacent about anything that concerned her siblings, had been the guiding star of her life. She'd always known it sat on her shoulders to provide a model to base their characters on, to show them how to move forward and upward in society, and to protect them.

She imagined those would weigh heavier on her shoulders when she moved to Wylder but that couldn't be further from reality. Out here, both sisters seemed to require little guidance. Violet had grown into an accomplished woman and Daisy looked well on her way to doing the same.

Of course, the writing obsession was still entirely unsuitable, but Lily hoped a nice man might send those notions packing.

Her sister emerged from the house with the packet beneath an arm and a smile on her face.

"I'm glad you mentioned an outing." The other woman straightened her reticule on her wrist and took the packet in hand. "I had practically fallen asleep over Hamlet, to tell the truth."

"You wouldn't be the first to snooze over Hamlet, Claudius, and Ophelia. And I'm sure you wouldn't be the last, either!" She took a step from the porch onto the walkway. They walked to the gate, which she pulled open so her sister could go before her.

As she closed it behind them, she noticed two men on horseback ride by. They looked familiar but that couldn't be. She didn't know hardly anyone here, so how could she recognize them?

"I don't know, Lily. I think you're being kind. I don't imagine you've ever fallen asleep while reading one of the classics."

They turned toward town and she took the opportunity to link her arm with her sister's. All her life she'd watched her younger sisters act as close as a litter of kittens, but she'd held back. Now might be the time to strengthen the bonds of sisterhood she'd never managed to grow.

"You give me far too much credit. I have lost many moments to sleep when I should have been reading, especially on the side porch in Charleston. That wide wicker rocker always lulled me into a snooze."

A pang of homesickness, remembering the cozy spot where they all congregated.

How things had changed.

"Oh, that rocker." Her sister sighed. "I miss so much from home, including that magical chair."

"We mustn't get ourselves sad over being far from home. Why, we must remember that we've been given a chance to spread our wings, like baby birds. I bet there are lots of women back in Charleston who'd give their best dresses for an opportunity like this."

Buggies and wagons rumbled in the street, sending

up dust clouds. They both hid their faces in their shoulders as one passed. When the dust settled they continued walking.

"You're right." Daisy touched her free hand to her hair. Of all the sisters, she had been blessed with the most gorgeous locks. Thick and curly, they were the envy of the others—including Lily. "I'm sure they would. I'd like to get this to the post office before we walk about town if you don't mind. That way I won't have to carry the parcel and it won't get covered with dust before it even begins its journey."

The post office, a smallish building set beside the telegraph office on Old Cheyenne Road came into view when they turned the corner. Things were busy here down by the railroad tracks.

They stepped out of the path of a wagon. Then they crossed the street.

"Of course I don't mind." She paused, then met her sister's gaze. "But tell me, why do you persist in reading books that don't interest you? Hamlet isn't the first one that's bored you silly. Why do it?"

They climbed the steps in front of the post office and stood on the small wooden porch. The place lacked charm but at least the town offered postal service. Lily had been certain that wouldn't be the case so this came as a pleasant surprise.

Daisy met her gaze and shrugged. The lovely green dress matched her eyes, which were now very earnest. "I think that if I'm going to improve as a writer I should study the great authors. I don't dream I'll ever be Shakespeare, but I'm sure I can learn from him."

Lily took a letter from her pocket and held it out. For once, words eluded her.

Her sister accepted the letter to home, then turned and went inside the building.

It crossed her mind that her younger sister's commitment to writing remained serious.

Chapter 29

Ambling about town gave Lily the opportunity to finally get her bearings.

Wagons rattled up and down Buckboard Alley, some loaded with filled burlap sacks and wooden crates from the supply company on the corner. They avoided stepping in front of the laden vehicles, keeping to the side of the street and pointing out items of interest.

Maybe her active imagination gave Daisy the ability to see more than wood structures. She had a theory about what went on behind the front door of nearly every building they passed. How she thought of such wild things without any time to ponder mystified her older sister. She did, however, find the running commentary amusing.

"See that one? With the two grimy windows upstairs?" Her sister pointed with her chin, rather than a fingertip, as any well-bred woman would. "There's a card hustler living up there, hiding away from daylight. He only emerges after dusk, and then he slinks along in the shadows, all the way to the saloon, where he increases his wealth by duping unsuspecting cowboys out of their wages."

She surveyed the windows her sister indicated. They looked completely unremarkable, but she played along with the narrative.

"What does this cheating fellow eat? He must be

starved by sundown."

The other gave a slow nod. "Good of you to be considering the man's hunger. Honestly, I wouldn't've thought you'd care so much but you're right, he is ravenous by sundown. But he dines well at the saloon and when no one's looking he fills his vest pockets with sandwiches, so he'll have something to eat the following day."

Culpepper's Boarding House stood at the far end of the street.

She tipped her head to the big building. "What about that place? I imagine it's got all sorts behind its windows."

"Indeed, it does. A boarding house is the scene of so many dramas, they're almost too numerous to discuss."

She did not attempt to conceal her amusement. As she leaned close, she threaded her arm through Daisy's. "But I'm sure you can muster the effort to regale me with stories, can't you? Why, sister, you've never failed at whipping up a tale."

The other woman stopped walking and turned to meet her gaze. The luminous green eyes that had sparked conversation since her birth held open amazement.

"Lily, I have never seen you so…well, so, ah… It's just that you're usually not this, ah…"

She pulled her brows together. "What? Spit it out."

"Sisterly!" Her younger sister placed her free hand over her mouth as her eyes rounded. "I'm sorry, that probably didn't sound very nice at all, but you must admit, you don't generally lark around with any of us. And me, never. Let's not be shy about it, you barely tolerate me most days."

The fun swept out of her like air leaving a balloon. When she tried to pull her arm from Daisy's, the other held firm.

"No, you won't get away like that, Lily. I know I made a huge mess of it but I'm trying to tell you that I like this…this sisterly fun makes my heart happy. I've always wished we could be this way."

She swallowed around a lump that appeared without warning in her throat. She didn't have the glibness of the other and words didn't burst into her head. A nod, for now, and she took a step forward keeping her arm in her sister's.

Shame washed over her. The truth in the other's words were like a slap, but they were well-deserved. Partly, at least. She may have been less kind to the others but her stance as the first-born female in the family dictated she provide an example for them. That sense of duty was one of the things their parents had instilled in her, right from the moment her first sibling had been born. She carried the responsibility every day of her life along with the knowledge that she did her best not only for her sisters, but for Mother and Father, as well.

She had been harsher than necessary, though—and she realized it now. Whether the western climate or her delicate condition worked to change her attitude, she did feel a sense of kindness to the others that hadn't been within her before.

Still, Daisy's declaration of her non-sisterly behavior prior to this move prickled her. A bit. But not nearly as much as it would have a month ago.

She recognized the hopeful tone in her sister's

voice when she spoke again. "Look, Lily, the hotel. It's pretty grand for a small town, don't you think?"

They'd turned onto Wylder Street and stood across from the Wylder Hotel.

"It is. It surprised me that the place has a hotel at all, but I never thought to see one this large." She gazed toward the upper windows, sweeping her attention over the flowerboxes dripping pink and red blooms, and nodded. "Certainly grand in this setting." She paused and looked over at her sister. "Maybe some time you'll tell me stories about what's going on in there."

The other woman's lips rose at the corners. "I'd like that, sister. Very much."

"It's settled then." She swallowed hard. That pesky throat lump threatened to reappear. To their right, the mercantile. "How about we splurge on a few pieces of hard candy? My throat isn't liking this dry climate and dust much. Something sweet will soothe, I think."

Chapter 30

When Lily stepped through the front door of Wylder's mercantile, she felt instantly at home. A cheery atmosphere made the store snug, despite the size of the building. A sweet scent wafted toward her. She couldn't put a finger on what she smelled, but it reminded her of Charleston.

The space loomed large before them and merchandise hung from the ceiling and on the walls. Baskets overflowed with colorful items. Goods of all types and for all purposes, it seemed, were on display.

Daisy turned to her and grinned. "It reminds me of Babbitt's Mercantile, on Charleston Street. Not as fancy, but it gives a nice feeling when you walk in, doesn't it?"

She'd been thinking the same thing. Babbitt's lived in her heart, almost as close as if it were a family member. Their childhoods included endless trips to the big store, with its intriguing displays and wide glass-front candy counter.

"Think they have peppermint sticks here?" She looked toward the center of the store, where a tall man stood behind the counter. There were baskets of small treats near him and she suspected the candy might be there, too.

"I sure hope so. Father's promise of one for the walk home is the single thing that kept me from running my fingers through the pencil basket and grabbing a handful every time we went into Babbitt's." Her sister raised an eyebrow at her. "I know he kept me from indulging my writer's overindulgence that way. What did he keep you from?"

She considered. What exactly had she coveted as a child? "I suppose that I'd have to say he kept me from asking to buy household items. You know, stirring spoons and thread to make doilies." She shrugged. "I always wanted a home of my own, to choose curtains and plan meals. So the candy promise kept me from lingering in the aisles where I had no business."

"I've yearned to be an author and you a wife." Daisy put a hand on her shoulder and gave a squeeze. "Funny how two children raised in the same house could be so different."

"No telling what will land in a small child's heart, I guess." She took a step forward. "I hope we both get what we want out of life."

"Me, too." Daisy followed her deeper into the store. "And I hope they have peppermint sticks here. It seems they have everything else, doesn't it?"

It certainly did seem that way. She headed for the far end of the store, to see what Wylder's mercantile offered. There weren't any pressing needs now, but one could never tell when something might come up.

Jars of unsharpened colored pencils lined a shelf. Beside them, fabric-covered journals. She ran a finger over the small books, wondering what color to choose.

"Uh oh. Has my writing passion influenced you?" Her sister's tone teased. They both knew better.

"Not quite." She reached for a book with a blue floral cover, then chose a half-dozen pencils in assorted hues. "I thought Alexia might like one. She told me she'd like to write, so why not encourage that?"

"You're kind, sister. I'm sure the girl would appreciate it. After all, her mother is gone, and she might need a little extra attention."

This newfound closeness made Lily's heart swell. Not being at odds or having to remind anyone of the rules of conduct gave her ease she'd never felt before.

So much had changed in such a short time.

They were about to make their way to the counter when a female voice from the next aisle caught her attention. She heard their sister's name mentioned, so she put a hand on Daisy's arm.

"Violet Bloom is one wise woman. Came to town, found her intended dead, and wasted no time scraping up a new man. Gotta hand it to 'er, she did good." The voice did not ring a bell with Lily, but she had not met enough of Wylder's citizens to get to know many people.

The woman made no effort to conceal the conversation. Her gossipy tone gave Lily the impression that she enjoyed spreading news about others. A hint of glee tinged every word.

The woman continued, her voice lifting on the mention of the man associated with Violet. "And she fell into it, she did. That Harvey fellow is one of the richest around, I hear. Runs some kind of money office that caters to mining companies, owns that fancy house, comes from big wealth back east is what I heard."

The voice that replied sounded muffled, as if the speaker held a hand near her mouth. Still, she overheard enough but before she could walk around to the next aisle, the woman went on in an even louder tone of voice.

"I hear his brother's got pockets filled with gold, too—and he's not spoken for although one of the sisters, the new ones in town, looks to have her sights on 'im. Could be her sister told her he's loaded, like 'is brother."

The words apparently carried to her sister because Daisy whirled around, her mouth wide open. She looked like a fish on a pier and would have brought a giggle had she not been trying to conceal their presence. Lily placed a finger over her lips, urging the younger sister to remain still. The jaw snapped shut but the green eyes remained enormous.

The louder one spoke again. "Well, all I can say is, if you have any thoughts to catchin' that Theo Harvey for yourself, you'd best move on him. Otherwise the Bloom sisters'll swoop in and grab his wallet—ah, heart, too."

The two women shared a laugh, she supposed over the last line, before walking toward the back of the store. They were middle-aged, dressed conservatively, and wore hats that concealed their faces.

Lily's face burned. She nearly followed the women, to see how they'd act when they came face-to-face, but she resisted. Better to hold her head high and avoid the gossipers.

"Come on, let's get out of here." Daisy gave her a gentle nudge toward the front of the store, and she didn't resist.

The man behind the counter smiled. He stood tall and thin, with light brown hair and gentle eyes.

"Nice to see the Bloom sisters made it to Wylder safely. I know your sister has been looking forward to your being here for a while. She must be happy to finally have some family out west with her."

"Why, that's kind of you, Mister Wylder. Yes, we're glad to be here with our sister. She's been missed." She handed over her selections and opened her reticule to pay.

He wrapped the pencils in brown paper and tied the bundle with string. His fingers were long and thin, and they worked while he spoke. The book got the same care. "Can I get anything else for you ladies?"

Her sister cleared her throat, the way she would have when they were children.

She took the lead and pointed to the candy display. "We'd like five peppermint sticks, please. If you'd be kind enough to wrap one separately, I'd be grateful." She'd tuck that one in with Alexia's other things, to make a nice gift for the girl.

Chapter 31

The packages were tucked beneath her arm. They'd wait to enjoy the candy until they were home, to save themselves from having it covered in road dust. Besides, despite being in the west, there were social standards to be observed. They couldn't very well mosey through town sucking on candy sticks like two schoolgirls.

Lily tipped her head toward a small building across the street. It appeared to have two businesses in it. The sign that said Mining Office—T. Harvey caught her eye.

"That must be where Thomas works." She slowed, to get a good look at the place, but there wasn't much to see. The building looked well-kept, with a good roof and painted siding. A window box overflowed with blue wildflowers.

"Looks respectable." Her sister tilted her head and added, "Not exactly the brick-front buildings we're used to, but it's certainly not bad at all. I really expected there to be tumble-down buildings and rotting carcasses out here. This is not what I thought it would look like in Wylder."

She shook her head. "You do have quite the imagination. Rotting carcasses, indeed! But if that's what we found I would've had all three of us on the next stagecoach back to civilization."

"Then it's a good thing we didn't find any of that." Daisy giggled.

"It is."

They walked slowly. Without a destination or schedule, the leisure to look into windows, admire displays, and soak in the town's flavor afforded them time to dawdle.

She tried to note the shops that might come in handy for future reference. If she were going to make her home here, she needed to stop relying on Violet for directions. She had to find her own way.

A thought had worried her mind for the past few days. Now, she broached the subject.

"I'm thinking that I can't stay with Violet indefinitely. I mean, you can, being younger and all, but it doesn't seem quite right for me to impose on her in that teeny house for too long."

The other woman stopped dead in her tracks. When she turned to face her sister, the look on her face left no room for interpretation. She'd shocked her to her core.

"You can't be serious. Mother and Father would want us to stick together—the Bloom sisters, we aren't meant to be separated."

If she'd thought the topic would cause such distress, she'd have kept it to herself. But they were already in the thick of it with no turning back now.

"Our parents would want me to make my own way, to find a place that is large enough to offer my sisters shelter if they ever need it. They would expect me to decide what to do with my life and find a reputable way to make a living." When she said it out loud, it sounded overwhelming. "That's what I plan to do."

"We're all finally beginning to behave like sisters.

Why can't that be enough for now?"

She took a deep breath but kept the truth from emerging from her mouth. The house couldn't accommodate one more person and in no time there would be another Bloom in this world. The reality of her situation couldn't be ignored for long.

But upsetting Daisy on such a nice day, when they were getting along so well, served no purpose. She patted her sister's hand and urged her to walk forward.

"You're right. Pay no attention to me, thinking out loud that way. Let's change the subject."

The other woman didn't need any urging. She dropped her head closer and lowered her voice. "Did you hear those two women? I wish I'd gotten a look at them, but I bet I'll recognize the loud one's voice if I hear it again."

"Impossible not to hear them. And me, too. I'll know her by her voice." She shook her head. They'd come to the end of the wooden walkway, so she stopped and scanned the street. A few wagons rumbled in the distance, but safe to cross here so she stepped out. "Horrid the way they gossiped like that, right in the middle of the mercantile where anyone could hear them. Let's not say anything to Violet. There's no reason to upset her."

"I agree. She doesn't need to know she has neighbors who are—"

A horse pulled up a few feet in front of them. Beside it, a second horse. Their sudden appearance caused both women to stop in the middle of the street.

She looked up and instantly recognized the pair. They were the ones Theo chased off his land. In town, they looked as dirty and disagreeable as they had at his place.

Unhurried movement inched her right hand down her side and into her skirt pocket. When her fingers wrapped around the small pistol she took a deep breath.

"Well, lookee here." The man spat a stream of tobacco juice into the street. "If it ain't the pretty lady that was standin' on a porch recently."

She tugged on Daisy's arm. "Come on, this way."

They walked to the side, hoping to go around and continue on, but the men urged their horses to move forward.

Heat flooded her cheeks. How dare they impede their movement—and right on the main street in broad daylight. This could not be tolerated.

She squared her shoulders and met the spitting man's gaze.

"You are in our way. Please move so we can get by."

He snorted, a disagreeable noise. The expression on his pock-marked, grimy face scared her. His eyes were dark and blank, as if he didn't have one ounce of feeling in him.

"Now is that any way to talk to a friend?"

"We are not friends, sir. Now please let us pass."

She tried to step around them and again they moved their horses two feet ahead.

Daisy opened her mouth to speak but Lily cut her off. These men didn't have ears fit to hear her sisters' voices, and she wouldn't allow it now.

"You must let us pass or I will go for the sheriff."

"Well, now ain't that somethin' to be afeared of." He turned to the silent man, who sneered. "Looks like the lady has more gumption than her man."

"I'm going for the sheriff." She took a step back. The law office might be anywhere in this little town, she had no way of knowing, but it didn't matter. They needed to get away.

"Now wait a minute, don't go gettin' your britches in a twist. No need for that. Just let your man know that we aim to sell that land next to his and he'd better get used to the idea." He spat again. "Or else!"

The two men turned their horses and, without one backward glance, rode down the street toward the boarding house. She wondered if they were staying at Culpepper's and thought of going to find the sheriff to tell him what happened. Then she pushed it all aside. They weren't in Charleston anymore. She'd best get used to that, fast.

"Lily, who were those vile men?" Her sister's eyes were, thankfully, not fear-filled but angry. "They were disgusting—and how dare they hold us up like that?"

She urged her sister toward the other side of the street. A wagon lumbered their way, and she didn't want to be caught in the middle any longer.

"They were out on Theo's property when he took me to see his place. It seems there's a piece adjacent to his that's exceptionally nice and has some interest." She thought it must be truly special to have caught this much attention. "They were ornery with him, but worse with us. Again, I don't think you should say anything to Violet. I don't want her to worry."

"I won't but you have to promise to stay away from them."

"Oh, no worries there. I'd like to never see them again as long as I live."

They strolled the far side of the street, scanning

storefronts once more. She wanted her sister to put the unfortunate experience out of her mind but being unfamiliar with town she couldn't guess which store would provide a diversion.

As luck would have it, she saw Lin step out of a small shop to their left. The pretty woman looked up and down the street and smiled when she spotted them.

"Oh, two of the Bloom sisters. So nice to see you in town."

Lily glanced at the sign above the door. Wei's Gemstones.

The door opened and a Chinese man stepped out. Trim, handsome, with big brown eyes and a wide smile, he stopped beside Lin.

"I saw you from inside my shop and had to come meet you. I see the family resemblance and know that you must be the two newly arrived Bloom sisters." He tipped his head in greeting. "I am Liu Wei, at your service."

His manners were impeccable and made Lily feel entirely at ease.

She nodded. "It is our pleasure to meet you, Mister Liu. I'm Lily and this is my sister, Daisy."

He nodded to each, met their gazes, and smiled. "Two more beautiful flowers to add to Wylder's garden. I am very honored to meet you both."

His gaze lingered on hers for a long moment and in that instant it felt as if the man could see beneath her skin. The sensation surprised her. A small smile played around the corners of his lips.

"It's nice to meet you, too, but we should get going." Daisy threaded her arm through Lily's and gave a gentle tug. "Shouldn't we, sister?"

Chapter 32

Lily looked around the schoolroom. Pride in her sister's devotion and hard work shot through her and she wished their mother were here to see this. Their parents would be pleased. She made a mental note to tell them of her visit to the schoolhouse in this week's letter home.

"I have to admit, I didn't expect anything this nice." She looked to a table in front of a window. Little pots of flowers bloomed, brightening the room and adding a cheerful air to the place. "You've really outdone yourself here."

Violet swept her hand across the edge of her desk and smiled. "Thank you for saying that. I know it's not Charleston, but I'm quite content. This is more than adequate to accommodate our needs."

"I'd say it is. Why, you've got everything you want, all the way out west. It's nothing short of a miracle if you ask me." She meant it, too. The education system did not let these frontier families down. This arrangement offered children opportunity to learn in a safe space. She could only imagine what some of the frontier homes looked like. This had to be a refuge for a lot of children. "You've done well for yourself, sister. I'm proud of you."

The other's eyes widened. She stared, then shook her head. "Why, I don't even know what to say. Thank you, Lily. That is the nicest thing you've ever said to me."

She crossed the room and put an arm around her sister's shoulders.

"I know, and I'm sorry." She took a deep breath. Tears prickled the backs of her eyes, but she ignored them. "I don't know what's come over me but I'm starting to realize that I've been a bit…well, I have had a tendency to…um, I guess I may have been a tad…"

"Bossy?"

She met her sister's gaze. The violet eyes held no malice, so she nodded.

She shot a look toward the wall behind Violet. A chalkboard with a quote by Shakespeare across the top of the black surface. Above the board, hand-lettered cards showing the alphabet. She saw a lot of hours and hard work behind the finer touches in this schoolroom. Again, a surge of pride in her sister's capability warmed her heart.

"Maybe a bit. But you've got to understand, it's fallen to me as the eldest to carry the weight of setting a good example and making sure you all toed every line. I had to do it. I couldn't haphazardly shirk my sisterly responsibilities, could I?" They didn't understand the obligations of being the eldest. They never would, either. "It was my place in the family to take the lead in every way. I did what I had to do."

Her sister nodded. "I see your point. It must have taken a toll to never be able to scamper about, the way we could. I know Mother expected more of you."

At least someone realized.

"I had a lot of jealous moments, watching all of you dash through life while Mother pressed me to act older than my age." She heaved a sigh. What sense did it make, going over these ancient slights? They were behind them and no longer held her captive. "But that is all in the past. Let's forget it if we can."

Violet pursed her lips, folded her hands and held them by her waist, and tilted her head. She looked every inch the schoolteacher. "I do want to know why you've had a sudden change of heart. Why are you so much less…ah…"

"Bossy?" She grinned. "I don't know, actually. Maybe it's being away from Charleston or even my, ah, condition. Whatever it is, I feel a burden has been lifted and I'm grateful for it."

They stood in silence for a long moment.

"I am, too." Violet spoke softly. "What are you going to do about your condition, sister? I've told the others they are not to badger you, but to give you space, so we haven't mentioned it. But since you brought it up, what will you do?"

Another glance around the schoolroom. Her gaze paused on a colorful picture that hung near Violet's desk, but no inspiration came to give her direction. She shrugged. "What can I do? It can't be undone, or if it can be I'm not willing to do that. I will let nature take its course and deal with the future as best I can."

There wasn't any other option open that she could see.

"You have sisters, you know. You're not alone."

That sweet sentiment came from the heart, she knew. It wouldn't do, though, to throw her sisters' reputations in a bad light by showing up with a fatherless child. She couldn't do that to them. Mother remained in Charleston, but she'd pounded the eldest's responsibilities in hard enough that Lily knew she had to break from the other two before the baby came.

"I know. Thank you for that. But let's not talk about it anymore." She looked around. "Are you all done here?"

"I am. We can head home and see what Daisy and Lin are doing. I wouldn't be surprised if they already have dinner planned out and half cooked."

She got the feeling that Lin kept the home fires burning for Violet and made her life here easier. How she'd misjudged the woman upon her arrival in Wylder embarrassed her.

"I'm glad you have such a kind person living with you. Tell me, are she and the man who owns the gemstone shop involved? They looked comfortable together, although neither showed any sign of improper behavior. I simply got a feeling when I saw them that there might be more to their friendship."

The other woman smiled as they walked toward the door. "You have excellent intuition. Yes, they are keeping company, but they are very private about it. The friendship is blossoming and it's nice to see Lin so happy. She deserves that, after all that's happened to her."

They stepped outside onto the small square landing beyond the door. She waited while Violet secured the schoolhouse, then they stepped down onto the path.

"What do you mean, all that's happened?"

Her sister's lips pulled tight, and she closed her eyes for a moment. When she met Lily's gaze, her eyes were sad. "She came here with her brother, but he was murdered, leaving her alone in a place where she knew no one and didn't speak the language. Lin has no family, save us."

The magnitude of the other woman's situation dropped like a lead ball in her gut. How on earth did one deal with that? And Lin never presented a sorrowful demeanor. The woman smiled constantly, ever cheerful and accommodating.

Shame washed through her. How could she have been so ghastly to the woman?

"I can't imagine how horrible that is." They turned toward home, blending with the foot traffic on the street. Afternoons were busy with lots of people running errands before sundown. "I'm glad she has you—no, she has us. We are her family now."

If Mother heard her, she would be in for a talking-to but their mother sat at home, stuck in her own way of thinking and not ready to see beyond it. Besides, if their parents could meet Lin they'd see her as a wonderful person.

"Yes, we are." Violet linked her arm through hers. The schoolhouse was not far from home, so they did not hurry. "I'm glad you came to visit the school. I have wanted you to see it."

"I took too long to stop in, but I won't be a stranger, I promise."

A peal of laughter drew her attention.

Theo stood with a brown-haired woman across the street. Her hand rested on his arm and as Lily watched, the woman patted his jacket twice before running her palm down his arm toward his hand.

She felt the color drain from her face and for an instant she thought she might be sick. Her gut rolled but she swallowed hard. "Who is that woman over there?"

Her sister's tone hardened. "No one you need to

know. Her name is Elisa Holland and she is trouble. The woman arrived in town looking for a husband and she won't be satisfied until she finds one."

Theo glanced across the street and met her gaze. His eyes grew and he pulled his arm out from beneath his companion's grasp. When he did, the woman tilted forward, falling against him hard enough that he put his hands out to catch her.

Lily's blood simmered as she quickened her footsteps. "Looks like the search is over."

Chapter 33

Violet's home offered a small porch overlooking the back yard. She had two trees, a vegetable patch, and tidy flower beds lining the walkway. A hitching post and small wooden structure that Lily supposed held wood filled the remainder of the space.

Peaceful—and out of sight. She sat there now with her feet propped on an upturned basket. Thinking came easily in the quiet atmosphere. She still heard wagon wheels and the occasional stubborn mule, but she felt hidden and that's what mattered.

Her sisters would fall under malicious gossip if they were too strongly associated with her when she had the baby. She would not put them in that predicament. By her estimate, she had a few months before her condition became apparent. Time enough to plan and relocate.

The door opened, then closed, when Violet stepped out. She sat on the other chair and put her feet on the wooden railing.

"No one tells you that teaching is hard on the feet. Oh, some days they ache so." She turned and grinned. "But when they do I sit back here, grateful Mother can't see me, and put them up for a bit. Works like a charm."

"I won't tell your secret. After all, you're keeping one of mine." A long sigh escaped her, dropping her shoulders down. "They will be so disappointed when they learn what's happened. Me, the one they held up to the highest standards, bringing shame on them."

The other woman shook her head. "It's a baby, not a train robbery. And women have been in this way from the dawn of time, sister. You need to be kinder to yourself and allow that you're human—and that this didn't happen on its own. Are you ready to talk about it? I assume it's Warren, isn't it?"

"Yes, it's Warren. But no, I'm not ready to discuss it and I'm not sure I ever will be." A small black-and-white bird landed on the railing beyond the basket near her feet. It hopped a bit then turned its black eyes on her and stared. She addressed her words to the newcomer. "And no, I'm not giving details, no matter how hard you press."

The bird fluttered its wings before taking off.

"Well, I guess you told him," Violet teased. She placed her hands together and flapped them, imitating a birds' wings. "Wouldn't it be great if we could chase off all our troubles that way?"

Silence fell between them, the comfortable kind that she had no desire to spoil by speaking. More birds came by, settled, and then flew off. The sound of a horse whinnying reached them. Leaves rustled in one of the trees.

It all reminded her of being at Theo's homestead, where the air kissed her cheeks and smelled so sweet. Solitude brought serenity, and she'd felt it there.

Her sister cleared her throat. "Theo stopped by. I told him you weren't available to visitors, the way you asked, but I have to tell you he looked saddened when I said it. The man cares for you, Lily, I know he does."

"Well, it looks like he's spreading that caring

nature around town, doesn't it?" She sounded like a scorned woman and didn't like it, but the words tumbled from her lips before she could stop them. "That sounds awful, I know. I can't be caught up with a man who talks up every female in town. Besides, once he learns of my condition he'll drop me like a hot potato, so what's the point?"

"He could think the child his own, couldn't he?" Her sister turned to her and lifted an eyebrow. "What man wouldn't love a beautiful child?"

"You mean…"

A nod. "I do."

"Violet! What would Mother say?" The very idea almost shocked her as much as the fact she'd gotten pregnant to begin with.

The eyebrow rose still higher. "She'd say that a woman should do whatever it takes to make a secure life for herself and her child, that's what. It's a hard place for women, this western frontier. We need to pull together and if that means turning the tables on men every now and again, so be it."

The younger sister had certainly grown up. Admiration made her heart warm as she reached a hand across the space between them to grab Violet's.

"When did you get so worldly, little sister?" The smile pulled her lips high at the edges and chased some of the gloom from her mind. "I'm proud of you."

Her sister gave her hand a squeeze, the way she had when they were children.

"Not all learning takes place in a schoolroom."

"Or teaching, either. You've just schooled me, out here on this porch."

Chapter 34

Lily refused to see Theo for two days. She heard his knocks on the door, saw his horse tied to the front gatepost from an upstairs window, and heard his voice carrying up the stairs when he implored her sisters to persuade her to see him.

To his credit, they tried. More than once. But she had her mind set.

Fleeing South Carolina because a man had broken his vow should have taught her a lesson. Apparently, she didn't learn as quickly as she thought she did.

She'd arrived in Wylder, fallen under the spell of another man almost immediately and, she had to admit, lost her heart. And this time, things were different.

Warren had been a convenience, but Theo worked his way into her soul, claimed a bit of her she hadn't realized existed, and had given her hope for a peaceful future. Her chest ached thinking about how she'd believed in him and the fantasies she'd had about the life they might build together.

But she'd been wrong. Again. There wouldn't be another ill-fated dalliance with her emotions. She wouldn't allow it. No, better to send him on his way now, than let him shatter the heart he'd already managed to wound.

Being homebound for days did nothing for her disposition. The others urged her to go to town with them, but she put them off. How could she be certain they wouldn't arrange to steer her toward a spot where Theo might be? She couldn't take the chance.

They'd all left early so the house sat silent.

Violet taught at the schoolhouse while Lin and Daisy ran errands in town. They'd mentioned picking up dinner supplies from the mercantile. They would be on Wylder Street which meant the other side of town might be sister-free—and a spot for getting some fresh air without being urged to give a certain man an audience.

She grabbed her reticule and bonnet and headed for the door. No one would be the wiser if she hurried. With any luck she'd be home before the others returned and would act as if she'd spent the day reading on the back porch, the same as she'd done for the past few days.

A warm breeze kissed her cheeks as she tied the bonnet's ribbons beneath her chin. She threw Mother's advice to the wind and lifted her face to the sky. So much joy in feeling heat on her skin—it seemed silly to deprive herself of such pleasure.

She set off toward town. Eagerness made her feet move quickly, sending a rush of excitement through her. Finally, to be out and on her own, without having to answer to anyone or do anything save what she wanted. Freedom felt glorious, and she breathed in its invigorating scent.

Reaching the far side of town meant passing near the end of Wylder Street. With any luck, no one would notice her.

There were wagons and riders in the streets and enough foot traffic for her to blend in. She glanced toward the mercantile. No sign of Theo or any of her sisters.

A look across the street. Lin and the gemstone dealer stood with Daisy and a man Lily had never seen before. They were in front of the gemstone shop, in a space out of the way of passing riders.

The group looked comfortable together, laughing and talking with familiarity. The man beside her sister wore blue jean trousers with a white shirt and brown leather vest. That he wore white on a weekday made an impression. He must have the means to keep a clean wardrobe. Many of the men she'd seen out here wore darker colors to hide dirt.

His build did not give his occupation away. He could have been banker or rancher, with a broad back, wide stance, and slim hips. Her gaze lowered to touch on his buttocks. The man was certainly well put together.

He leaned toward Daisy, and it occurred to her that the man's hair color matched her sister's almost perfectly. It touched his shoulders, a smooth fall of chestnut brown with golden highlights. She wondered what a child of the two would look like, and whether its locks might grow straight or curly like her sister's.

She shook the thought from her head. With a final glance, she turned toward the schoolhouse but kept to the opposite side of the road. Violet should be inside, but one couldn't be too careful.

A woman she'd met at the mercantile nodded as she passed. "Mornin', Miss Bloom."

Lily tipped her head and smiled. "Good morning."

There were too many new faces and unfamiliar names for her to give much thought to matching them, but it seemed that this woman might be one of the ladies whose children attended school. Milligan, maybe—with a half-dozen or so offspring. Yes, that must be it. She remembered the woman's name too late to use it but next time, she'd be prepared.

She surveyed the schoolhouse from a shaded position across the street. The bright building beamed like a beacon, inviting the town's youth to enter and learn. It melted her heart to see what her sister's presence in this rugged place meant. She softened the rough edges of frontier living by elevating minds. Lily resisted the urge to cross the street, dash into the schoolhouse, and tell Violet how proud she felt.

"Well, it's nice to see you again."

She whirled and came face to face with Gertie. The woman's last name did not come to mind but that didn't matter.

A smile, and a nod. "A pleasure to see you, too, Gertie. Beautiful day, isn't it?"

"Sure is. We love these spring mornings, before the summer heat sets in." She tipped her head toward the school. "Goin' in to see your sister?"

Lily took a step back, farther into the shadow of the building behind them. "No, not this morning. I just stopped to admire the place and, um…" She searched her mind for a reason to stand and stare. Her gaze fell on an object beyond the schoolyard. "Wondered about that wishing well. Seems unusual to have one of those, doesn't it?"

The other woman chuckled. "It sure does. Between us, the feller who built the thing was in the lead when tongues were handed out but most of what he said weren't fit for listenin'." She shook her head, sending a light brown curl bouncing on her ruddy cheek. The woman looked as if she hadn't led an easy life, but her eyes twinkled anyway. "Sure, he talked a lot but made no sense. Like that wishin' well. He insisted Wylder needed it and set about buildin' the fool thing, with his own money, supposedly."

"What happened to him? Does he toss coins into the well every day when he passes?"

The older woman snorted. "Hardly. Right after he put the last stone on the well, he died of throat trouble." She pantomimed being hung and added a small smile. "He had it comin'—seems the money he used for that silly thing and to buy property from a few people in town didn't rightly belong to him. On his way from New York he shot a man and stole every bit of his money. So he arrived here lookin' all fancy but when the law caught up with him we saw who he really was."

She looked over at the wishing well before turning back to Gertie.

"I guess that's how it is sometimes. We think we know someone, but we only see what they're willing to show us."

"Amen to that. Well, I'd best get moving. I'm headed to the mercantile for supplies for my pumpkin bread." The other woman squared her shoulders and gave a small smile. "It has a bit of a reputation around these parts, if I do say so myself. I'll bring one by your sister's place so you can taste it. Kind of a welcome to town gift."

"That's very kind of you, Gertie. Thank you. I'll look forward to it." She took a step away. "Nice seeing you this morning."

"You, too."

Lily passed the land office and made a mental note. It might be the place she'd have to visit to put in a claim. She'd decided to buy the land adjacent to Theo's. If it were even half as enchanting as his piece, it would offer a fine spot to raise her child.

She'd investigated the claims process. All she needed, a small structure and willingness to live on the land for a period of time, met her current situation. She had to get out of town, but not too far, so her sisters weren't adversely affected by their unwed sister's baby.

And if she were to stay in Wylder, which had always been her plan after Warren's dumping her, she needed to set up her own home. Away from the shadow of Violet's life. And close enough to oversee Daisy's.

Homesteading provided the ideal solution, and with the money left to her by Aunt Hilda, she had the means.

The land office would be tomorrow's errand.

Today, a walk in the sunshine without running into anyone else would suit her fine.

Chapter 35

Old Cheyenne Road did not match the busyness the merchant section of town offered. Here, the rail office and train depot were both deserted. Lily walked on the depot platform, sat in the shade for a few glorious, uninterrupted minutes, and surveyed the railroad tracks.

The Union Pacific passed through town. Laramie lay thirty-four miles to the west. Perhaps someday she might venture that far. Who could tell? It sounded like a good idea now, but her feelings changed so rapidly that when the time came she might not want to see the other town at all.

Don't worry about tomorrow, it'll come on its own time. Mother's words sang in her head. And while she knew Mother wouldn't be pleased with her eldest daughter's predicament, she still wished she had the chance to sit beside her and discuss the matter.

The time for motherly advice lay behind her. She had only herself for counsel now. Not the best option, but it would have to do.

Resolutely, she stood and continued walking. The tracks were silent, so she crossed them, taking care not to trip on the iron rails. On the far side, a feed store stood to the west, and it didn't elicit any interest, so she turned the other way.

A large building in the distance caught her eye so she headed for it. Perhaps some kind of refreshments were served there. Her throat felt parched from the heat.

As she drew closer to the building she saw open windows on the second floor, white lace curtains billowing from inside. Tinkling notes from a piano met her ears. The sound was light and fun, the sort of tune that made a toe tap. She caught a whiff of something sweet, a cinnamon-and-apples smell that reminded her of home.

She didn't see a sign on the building, so she walked around to the side. Maybe it had one of those hidden entrances, like some of the shops back home.

"Well, ain't this a nice surprise."

The voice knotted her stomach.

She looked up. The men from Theo's property, the spitting man and his silent friend. The quiet one put his horse on one side of her while the other stopped directly in her path.

"Let me pass." She thought about screaming but this side of the tracks didn't attract much traffic. She doubted the people at the feed store could hear her and who could tell if her voice would carry over the piano music coming from the nearby building? "Out of my way, please."

A stream of tobacco juice landed a foot from where she stood.

"Manners. I like that in a woman. Don't you, Wade?"

The man broke his silence in a voice that sounded like he borrowed it from a bear. "I told ya—don't use my name!"

The growl sent shivers up Lily's spine. The roar took him from quietly intimidating to ferocious in a heartbeat.

"She ain't gonna tell nobody." The talking man brought his horse so close she smelled the sweet odor coming from it and saw its withers move. "Why, there ain't nobody to tell where we're goin'."

He leaned out of the saddle and stretched an arm toward her.

Lily looked to the side. The man called Wade sidestepped his horse to bring her closer to his companion. Going forward would only bring her nearer to the dirty fingers that reached for her now.

She whirled and ran toward the animals' tails, toward the railroad tracks and the building just beyond it. Her skirt tangled around her ankles, and she wished she could wear blue jean trousers like men did.

"Help! Please, someone help me!"

A head appeared in an upper window. The woman looked half-clad but waved to her. "C'mon over, honey! We've got you!"

The breath from the man's horse hit her neck in a hot wave. A strong arm went around her waist and lifted her from the ground.

"Put me down!" She kicked but he laid her across his lap and held her there.

"Hey—let that lady go!" The voice coming from the sprawling building grew faint as the horse galloped away.

Lily wanted to jump off but knew the horse's hooves would trample her, so she held on and prayed they wouldn't take her too far. She had no way to get her bearings, no good ability to detect directions, and even if she did how far could a woman walk? This was not Charleston—the western frontier held all sorts of perils including snakes, nefarious men, native tribes who spoke languages she didn't understand, and so much more her head spun considering it all.

The only thing in her favor? The Remington over-under derringer in her skirt pocket. It gave her one chance to protect herself and she planned to use it.

Chapter 36

The lean-to consisted of two thick low-hanging cottonwood branches draped with pine boughs. It provided little shelter and no room to sit fully erect but at least it got Lily off the spitting man's horse. And she figured that the sooner they stopped, the closer they were to Wylder, so she didn't care about the accommodations.

The ride had been insufferable and more than once her captor's hand found its way to her bottom. She'd wanted to jump down and run but knew it wouldn't end well. The one attempt at flight when they'd grabbed her hadn't gotten her far.

Who could tell what consequences she'd face if she angered them? At their mercy, it felt best to cooperate until the opening to shoot one of them presented itself.

Her left wrist already had a red welt from the dirty, scratchy length of rope they used to tie her to the tree's thickest branch. She tugged at it whenever they weren't looking her way, hoping to somehow weaken the knot without bringing down the structure's roof onto her head.

Their horses nickered from beneath a nearby tree. They'd tied their mounts less thoroughly than they had her, so she planned to ride off on one when she got free.

"Whadda we do now? We can't keep her tied up like that forever." The one called Wade seemed less thrilled they'd kidnapped her than his partner did. He kept glowering at her, almost as if he wished she'd disappear. "We didn't need to take her."

The spitting one sneered. "Hell, we got ourselves a bargainin' chip in that there woman. We call the shots now."

"How do you figure?"

The man spat. Then he let out a laugh that sounded like a choking donkey and she wondered how much tobacco it took to make a man sound that way. The tail end of his laughter dissolved into a series of gurgles and gagging noises. They brought a smile to her lips, so she turned away. She didn't trust him not to hit her if he saw so she ducked her head to her shoulder for good measure. It didn't pain her one bit that he suffered an affliction.

"She were with Harvey, remember? The two of them was sittin' pretty out at his place, kissin' like newlyweds." The last he followed with a cackle.

The blood in her veins turned to ice. They'd spied on them! And she and Theo had assumed they were alone when they deepened their affection for one another.

"But how does that make any difference? What're we gonna do with her?"

She heard a twig crack behind the lean-to and realized they walked while they talked. She fixed her gaze on the ground in front of her and pretended to examine a leaf. Better if they believed she didn't hear their plans.

The spitting man snorted. Then she heard him spit. "We ain't gonna do nothin' with her. By now that soiled dove what saw us from the window of the Social

Club's got the sheriff's ear. She's yammering 'bout how a woman got herself picked up and rode off with. It'll take 'em some time to find her. By then, we'll be gone."

The stupidity of their plan nearly made her scream. It lacked everything, including a tangible result. The way it sounded, the disgusting man had scooped her up on a whim.

They'd traveled around to stand beneath a cluster of trees downwind of the shelter. Gratitude swept through her. The one man smelled worse than his horse, and any distance gave her belly a chance to settle.

She watched them through downturned lashes.

"What good does that do?" Wade slapped a hand against his thigh. Anger tinged every word. "We stole a woman just to let that sheriff find her? Shit, we'll be lucky if that Wylder fella don't get it in his head to come after us and string us up!"

"For what? Taking some long-toothed female? Hell, they's not worth anything. Asides, this one's built like a snake on stilts. She's past her prime and too tall for anyone to want her back—'cept Harvey, that is." He turned his gaze on her and narrowed his eyes. "We'll get his attention right quick. Should be enough to show him we mean business."

The frontier stretched out behind them. Dusty brown soil dotted with dried scrub. A tumbleweed spun off into the distance, headed for parts unknown in its own erratic way. A dust devil rose nearby, a sudden swirl of dirt rising into the hot air, then falling as suddenly as it appeared.

Lily wished she were still home on Violet's porch, her feet propped on that basket she used as a footstool.

This scorching heat and rugged terrain were bad enough, but she faced two horrible men who'd hurt her without giving it a second thought. She wasn't safe here—somehow she had to find a way back to that lavender house with its humble back porch and the loving family who were probably, even now, wondering where she'd gone off to.

Wade waved an arm toward her. "Why will he think that? It's not as if we're killin' her or anything."

The spitting man put a hand on the other's shoulder and grinned. She saw evil in the way he looked at her, so much that gooseflesh rose on her arms.

"Not this time, we ain't."

The next hours passed in a blur.

The men dozed beneath the trees near their horses, so she worked hard on the knots in the rope. The length they'd used was thick and its filthy knots had grown tighter from her pulling her arm away from the branch.

She considered shooting one of them, but which one? And if she missed she'd have both foul-tempered and bent on revenge. No, better to try to wiggle her hand out of the loop around her wrist, although blood ran down her forearm and the area felt as if bees stung her flesh.

Still, she tugged and twisted—and waited for a chance to run.

The sun dropped low in the sky. An afternoon chill crept into the air. She shivered and wished she'd never gone to town.

Hard to believe she'd been crouched beneath the pine branches all day. Her head, back, and legs ached. Her gut rumbled and her throat and mouth were so dry they felt glued closed.

Time dragged but she kept pulling on her arm. The shoulder throbbed now but the branch had begun to wobble. She looked toward the men, still prone beneath the trees. Then she checked the point where the branch met the shelter's roof. It showed signs of coming loose. She wondered how hard she'd have to yank to bring it down. She hoped her legs would hold when she tried to stand.

Wade sat up and put a hand to his eyes to scan the horizon. He stood, then kicked the other man in the thigh with the toe of his boot. "Get up. We got company."

The other rose and squinted toward the distance.

Lily followed their lead, but the side of the lean-to blocked her vision. She heard hoofbeats but they didn't seem close. The men, however, moved quickly.

"Hell, we wasn't supposed to sleep that long." Wade ran to the horses. He began to untie one's reins from a low-hanging branch. "We shoulda been long gone, damnit."

The other man spat. He tucked a chunk of tobacco into his cheek and held up a hand. "Now don't go gettin' yourself worked up. A change o' plans is all this is."

"Whaddaya mean?"

He pointed to Lily. "We'll take her with us, is all. Get a jump on 'em then let her go when we get far enough ahead." The men and horses were to the right of the shelter. He passed Wade and strode toward her. "C'mon, we got someplace to go."

Lily used every ounce of strength to pull against the support branch. A loud cracking sound split the air as branches fell on top of her.

"Hell, what's she doin'?" Wade sounded shocked that she resisted.

She threw her body toward the left side and prayed the thick branch wouldn't knock her unconscious. It didn't, so she crawled from beneath the boughs and came to her feet. Her legs were shaky, but she forced herself to run for the trees.

"Get her!" The spitting man yelled. "She's gettin' away!"

She heard thundering footsteps but didn't turn to look. Ducking low branches and scrambling over pinecones and brush, she ran between trees as if the devil himself were on her tail.

Her skirt hooked on a branch. She twisted and pulled until it tore, then she ran some more. The spitting man, with his wheeze and cough, fell behind but Wade pursued her like a weasel in a henhouse.

A tree root caught her toe, and she went flying. Pain shot up her ankle as she came down hard on her left shoulder. Before she could get to her feet, Wade grabbed her by the back of her skirt.

"I g-got you n-now, bitch!" His breath came in gasps, but his strength didn't seem affected by their scramble through the trees. He pulled hard on her skirt, flipping her over as if she were a fish lying on a sandy beach.

She landed on her back, the air forced from her lungs.

"Let go!" She kicked, but he tugged her toward him. "Stop it!"

Her hand clasped around the compact derringer, so she yanked it from her pocket and pressed the trigger. The flash startled her, but she pushed against him as the gun went off.

The man fell back, howling in pain, so she struggled to her feet and ran.

"You bitch—you shot me!"

Her ankle screamed but she forced herself to go on. It didn't matter that she couldn't move quickly—she put space between them and if it meant ruining her ankle for the rest of her life, so be it.

She ran for herself but also for the life inside her. There had never been more to protect than there was now, and she didn't intend to let anything happen to her child. Whatever it took, she'd keep her baby safe.

Chapter 37

Theo rode flat out, spurring his mount to move faster than the wind. The frontier stretched before him and while he had faith in the sheriff and his men, he couldn't rely on them to find Lily.

One of Miss Addie's girls had run to fetch the lawman after she witnessed two men abduct a woman. That he'd been near the jailhouse and heard the ruckus seemed a blessing. Had he been at the homestead instead of in town hoping to bump into the woman who'd caught his heart, he wouldn't have known anything about this. Worse, he wouldn't be able to offer to help find Lily.

The sheriff had sent two other pairs of men on the hunt. He'd taken one other fellow with him and had invited Theo to join their party, but it made sense that the more who spread out and searched, the better the odds of finding her. He didn't need help rescuing Lily. If he found the men responsible for carrying her off, he planned to tear them limb from limb. Slowly, so they suffered.

Damn, but loving a woman was harder than he thought it would be. He'd imagined hearts and flowers, and maybe even some social dances, but riding across the frontier as if Satan chased him had never entered his mind. No one mentioned this part of courting when they brought up the topic of finding a wife—and a good thing, too. This could frighten even a brave man away.

He reached the river and let the horse stop to drink. No sense killing the animal, especially when he crossed land on horseback more quickly than he did on foot. No, let the horse drink its fill, then he'd continue the search.

A native appeared on the other side of the river. They considered Medicine Bow River sacred, a place to make offerings and give thanks, and a spot of healing. The man sat astride a beautiful Appaloosa. He directed the horse into the water. They emerged a few yards downstream from where Theo sat on his mount.

The man rode nearer. When they were close enough to speak without shouting, he stopped.

He wore a faded cotton shirt, leather trousers, and moccasins on his feet. A seen-better-days bowler sat on his head and shaded his eyes. His long black hair hung in twin lengths down the front of his body to his chest. The ends of his plaits were tied with leather.

They nodded a greeting. The man might be Cheyenne or Arapaho, Theo couldn't be sure. But what mattered more than what tribe he belonged with was his willingness to help find Lily.

He wasted no time. "I'm looking for a woman. She's been abducted and I just want to find her and take her home." The man hadn't said a word, so he hoped he understood English. "Have you seen someone like that? A woman taken by two men, maybe struggling to get free?"

The other man looked into the distance for a few moments, then he met Theo's gaze and shook his head. "No. I have not seen the woman you search for." He tipped his chin to the water rushing by. "But I ask my ancestors to keep her safe until she is found."

Theo would have dismounted and shaken the man's hand if he weren't in such a hurry to find Lily. So many spoke badly about those who inhabited this land before the white man spread westward, but he'd never had any reason to do that. Every interaction, like this one, proved that men could be civil with each other and act in good faith, regardless of the color of their skin or place of birth.

He touched the brim of his hat and turned his horse. He'd look upstream a bit, then head back to Wylder. With any luck the sheriff had already rescued her.

"Thank you. I'm grateful for your help—and that of your ancestors, too."

Chapter 38

Lily waved away Daisy's offer to brew a fresh pot of tea.

"The one on the table is still warm. Also, if you all keep filling me with tea I might float off." She smiled at her younger sister. Since her return home, they had all be wonderfully considerate and caring. The three women had seen to her every need, with kindness and compassion, and she felt grateful beyond words. "But really, I am fine, thank you."

The other woman sat on the edge of the chair pulled up alongside the settee. They were in Violet's parlor and for the first time all day, she shared the space with only one other.

A fire burned in the hearth. Despite the warm morning, they all insisted she shouldn't catch a chill. Quilts lay near her feet, should she feel the need for covering.

On the table, every item one might desire during convalescence. Two books of poetry, a handkerchief, glass of water, teacup and saucer as well as the teapot, a note from Alexia and a card drawn with the pencils Lily sent to her, an orange, and a cup of freshly cracked walnuts. She could think of nothing they'd missed and felt as pampered as a spoiled housecat.

Her sister reached to take her hand, then pulled back.

Doc Sullivan had bandaged her wrist where the rope had taken the skin off. Lin's friend Mister Liu brought a salve made from herbs that the doctor approved and while it made the wound less painful, she would probably have a scar. The medical man had been apologetic when he told her so, but it did not matter to her. A visible reminder that she'd fought against those who tried to harm her was something she didn't mind carrying through life.

The scramble through brush and over rocks left her right hand a mess, too. No bandages there, only a coating of salve and watchful eyes to see that the cuts didn't begin to fester.

"I'm sorry. I want to comfort you, but I don't know how." Daisy's gaze went from wrist, to hand, to her face. "There are so few spots on your body that haven't suffered damage."

"You do comfort me. Being here, taking care of my needs, keeping me company during these past few days…it is a great help, sister."

The other woman grinned. "I guess we're even now. I mean, after the care you gave me when I had the miserable ague."

She laughed. For an instant, Daisy looked shocked by the sound, but she grinned, then joined in.

It had been days since they'd shared anything this joyful or comfortable.

"You're right, we are even now. I think you've all gone beyond the care I gave you, actually. I mean, when you were ill I didn't have to search for you." She shuddered. Nightmares plagued her these past few nights. Visions of being lost forever alone on the frontier would not leave her mind. "I'm so thankful you found me."

"We owe that to the woman from the Social Club. She ran for the sheriff as soon as you were carried off. We really need to do something to thank her."

Violet filled her in yesterday about the woman who worked for Miss Addie, the town's madam. The club provided a necessary service and while she wouldn't have guessed that's what the large building housed, she understood now why it had seemed so welcoming. She imagined it beckoned the men who frequented it, too. The music and delightful aromas wafting from its open windows would lure anyone in.

"I agree. When I'm on my feet I'll make a call to thank her personally." She didn't care whether her visiting a whorehouse would meet with anyone in Wylder's approval. The woman had saved her life, and she intended to show her gratitude.

"I'll go with you." Her sister raised an interested eyebrow. "Who knows? I might learn something useful for one of my stories. I heard yesterday that another one is being published in the fall. The magazine sent a check and everything."

Daisy had the heart of an author. Denying it proved useless so Lily took a deep breath, prayed their mother wouldn't ever find out she'd taken the younger sibling to a house of ill repute, and nodded.

"That would be nice, thank you. And congratulations on the story." She swallowed hard and met the other's gaze. "I am proud of you."

A knock came at the front door. Before Daisy could rise to answer it, Lin walked on silent feet past the open parlor doorway.

Low voices, then the sheriff appeared in the hall

outside the door. His hat hung from one hand and he wore a hopeful smile. "Miss Sun said you might finally be up to a visitor for a minute or two."

Her sister rose and waved him in. "I think it would be a nice change for her. I'm sure my sister grows tired of my incessant chatter." She smiled and went over to the fireplace. "Please, have a seat. I'll just add a log to this, then pick up my reading."

She dropped a length of wood in the fire. Then she sat on the hearth and opened the book sitting on the edge of the stones.

Branch Wylder entered with the air of a man who knew his business. He hadn't been sheriff for long, but he'd already gained the town's admiration and that included hers, too.

"How are you feeling, Miss Bloom? Better, I hope."

"Oh, yes, much better. It's been three days and each one brings less soreness." She gestured to her ankle, where it lay propped on a pillow. "I'll be glad when I can walk again, but I'm not complaining. Thank you for coming to my rescue."

He colored slightly. The man rubbed a hand across his chin and looked to the floor before meeting her gaze. "Just doing my job, ma'am. And I can't take all the credit. Why, if Miss Addie's gal hadn't come running to find me, I don't know how I would've found you. She's the one to thank."

She nodded. "I plan to. Now, Sheriff, what brings you here today? It's kind of you to stop by but I'm sure you have better things to do than call on invalids."

"I doubt you'll be down for long, Miss Bloom. I've seen how strong your sister is, and Miss Sun, too.

Women in this house aren't shrinking violets, and I'm sure you're not, either." A chuckle. The rasp in his voice made the man sound as if he'd spent countless hours around a campfire. "Want to let you know you won't ever be bothered by that pair of villains again. Couple of marshals showed up yesterday. Seems the pair is crooked enough to sleep on corkscrews. They've been pulling off shady land deals across more miles than I can count. Marshals will be taking 'em away later on."

Relief coursed through her. It had been on her mind that the two might give her trouble, especially when they saw she planned to put in her own homesteading claim. This eased her fears.

"I'm so grateful for your hard work. If not for your rescue, I shudder to think of what would have happened."

The lawman met her gaze. "Like I said, I was just doing my job. And it wasn't only me. Two pairs of men went searching for you. And Theo Harvey—he set off on his own to try to find you. Met himself a native down by the river, said the man asked his ancestors to watch over you. So it wasn't only me who was workin' to save you."

Theo. And a native? Down at the river?

She shook her head to clear it. So much had happened in so short a time, it hardly seemed real.

The sheriff got to his feet. "Well, just wanted to let you know about those two varmints. They're riding off to justice—and I don't think it's going to be pretty."

"Thank you for the news. I'm glad to hear it." She paused and pulled her brows together. "But, Sheriff Wylder, aren't they injured? How can they ride?"

He slapped his hat on his thigh. A smirk lifted the edges of his moustache. "Miss Bloom, we don't care if they're comfortable. Fact is, the harder the ride to justice is, the more we like it."

Chapter 39

Lily took the fresh handkerchief from Violet. She tucked it into her pocket and gave it a small pat. Newly decorated with delicate embroidery, it had taken her sister a week of work. Truly, an act of love.

"I'm glad you agreed to see Theo. He's been beside himself for days. If not for Thomas talking with him, I'm sure the man would've scaled the house and climbed in through your bedroom window." Her sister met her gaze. "He cares for you, you know."

She did know. But that would change when he heard her truth.

Saved from responding by a knock at the door, she took a deep breath and prepared for the upcoming visit. She didn't expect it to last long. Once he heard what she had to say, he would leave and never return. She only hoped he'd be kind enough to keep her secret.

Violet left to answer the knock, since the doctor still recommended rest for the expectant mother. Lounging on the settee bored Lily to tears but if it helped her body overcome its ordeal and kept the baby safe, she would endure.

Theo stood in the doorway, hat in hand and a smile on his handsome face. Her heart fluttered in recognition and her hands trembled. Lord, but the man turned her insides to jelly.

He met Lily's gaze. "You look, as ever, lovely. I

hope you're feeling better."

"I am." Her voice came out as a whisper, so she swallowed. "Thank you."

Two steps forward brought him into the room. He looked at the quilt at her feet and nodded. "That'll do."

"For what?"

"I hoped you'd consent to go on a short ride with me. I have my buggy outside."

Her sister had been standing in the doorway but now she stepped forward. "But she's in no condition to go out."

The man smiled and met Violet's concerned gaze. "I checked with Coyote, and he feels it would be the best medicine for your patient. Thomas helped me outfit the buggy so Lily will ride in absolute comfort." He turned back. "That is, if she'll consent to go with me."

What did she have to lose? Telling him they could not have a future together in this room, in her sister's house, did not appeal. Forever after there would be sad memories haunting the walls. Better to do it elsewhere.

She dipped her chin.

He didn't wait for more encouragement. Setting his hat on his head, he came close and lifted her in his arms. Her sister placed the quilt over his shoulder as he strode toward the door.

The sun touched her cheeks, and a gentle breeze blew the scent of hyacinths through the air. She wrapped an arm around Theo's shoulders and savored the moment.

His heart beat against her side, keeping time with her own.

When he reached the buggy, he set her down on the

seat with as much care as if she were a newborn babe. A footrest had been added to the rig, and he propped her legs on the cushioned area before settling the quilt across her lap.

"Is that comfortable?" His gaze met hers and in that instant she thought she could swim in their molten dark brown depths. A wrinkle appeared between his eyes. "Is there something you need? I'll get whatever you want, just say the word."

She shook her head, realizing she'd left the house without her bonnet or reticule. She had nothing but herself. Somehow, it seemed enough.

"It's perfect, thank you."

He went to the other side and climbed in. His shoulder brushed hers and sent shivers up her spine. A flick of the man's strong wrist, and the horse moved forward.

They did not speak during the ride. She thought he planned to take her to his property, where they had shared such magical moments, but he remained in town. They passed the school, land office, and livery.

The quiet did not bother her. The gentle clip-clop of the horse's hooves steadied her nerves. Her heart stopped hammering and somewhere near the town cemetery her jaw relaxed. It made no sense to agonize over this meeting. She expected it to be short, but not particularly sweet. Whatever happened, she had already survived a skirmish with her life intact. She would do the same now.

"Are you okay? Cozy enough?" His tone dripped concern. "You're not getting jostled, are you?"

She laid a reassuring hand on his arm. He felt warm and strong beneath her touch. "I'm fine. And it's good to be out in the fresh air, thank you."

Her wrist fared better when her hand sat in her lap, so she removed it from his arm. Doing so tugged at her heart, though.

A ribbon of water appeared before them, and she saw he directed the horse for it.

"What is that?" Trees lined the bank, dripping low to hang over the slow-moving water. The spot called to her, almost as if she'd been here before. It was silly because she had never seen the place, yet it felt familiar. "The water, I mean. What is it called?"

"Medicine Bow River." He pulled the horse up in the shade of a tree on the bank. The sound of water tumbling over stones and logs filled the air with music. "It's said to be a holy place, a special spot for the native people as well as the settlers."

She believed it. The air seemed alive, and she felt stronger than she had since her kidnapping.

"I love it here." She spoke the truth. "It feels like coming home."

He gave her a gentle smile. "I hoped you'd say that."

They did not speak for several minutes, and that, too, felt right.

Theo stretched an arm along the back of the buggy seat. He removed his hat and placed it beside him. She waited while he ran his free hand across his temple, brushing his hair off his face. The man was getting ready to talk and she had no plans to stop him.

Let him speak.

Then she'd tell him her secret.

And then he could drive her back to Violet's where they would part ways. Her heart broke considering it but there could be no other outcome.

"We need to talk. That's why I brought you out here." The deep timber of his voice sent butterflies flying low in her belly. She wondered if the baby felt them, too.

"I know."

He nodded. They both gazed at the water. It seemed easier that way. Looking at him only showed what she'd almost had—and what she was about to lose, so she kept her face turned to the river and concentrated on breathing.

"That day you saw me talking with that woman—"

"You don't owe me any explanations."

He sighed. "It's not a matter of owing. You need to understand that I know what it looked like, and I realize it must have hurt you, but honestly, there's nothing between me and her. I don't mean to badmouth the woman but every eligible man in town knows she's looking for a husband." He turned to face her and waited until she met his gaze. "I'm not interested in being her husband, Lily."

Maybe she should press him to take up with the eager female. He deserved a wife and family, and aside from the ear-splitting giggle the woman might not be bad.

"I don't understand why you think you need to tell me this." She tried to harden her heart, but it didn't cooperate. When he looked at her with tenderness, the way he did now, she wanted to throw her arms around his shoulders and bury her face in his neck.

"Remember when we agreed to be friends and tell each other the truth, always?"

A lump formed in her throat. She remembered. She

nodded, blinking to keep from crying.

"Well, I haven't been completely truthful with you, even though I said I would be, and I even said that I think women might not like the truth but they should hear it anyway." He ran a lazy finger across the top of her shoulder and turned to her. His gaze locked hers in its grip, the intensity searing into her soul. "This is the truth Lily: I'm in love with you. I know it hasn't been years of courtship but out here we don't have time to waste. Besides, I knew the minute you got off that stagecoach, all ornery, wearing that black stripe across your pretty face." He grinned. "You reached into my chest and grabbed my heart with that first scowl."

Her mind spun. His eyes, so dark and lovely. His voice. The words, a jumble in her head.

"I don't understand."

"There's only one thing to understand, honey. Do you love me, too? That's all that matters."

She swallowed. Time to come clean. There was more to understand than that.

"I'm pregnant."

His brows lifted. A fast glance toward her belly, then his gaze met hers again.

"Do you love the man?"

She shook her head. "No." Her mouth felt dry. "I love you."

It took a moment, but a slow grin spread across Theo's face. He leaned close, and she felt his breath on her cheek.

He placed a gentle hand on her neck and pulled her even closer. "Will you marry me, Lily?"

Her breath caught in her throat.

"But the baby, Theo."

The man's shoulders went up, then dropped. He shook his head and gave her a sweet smile. "I want lots of 'em. The sooner we hear the patter of little feet in that house, the better."

"Really?"

A nod. "Really. And I hear you're setting to buy the claim that butts up on mine. I can't let you spend your money. I think you should save that, but I have enough for us to lay claim to the parcel so we can increase our holdings. How does that sound?"

"Like Heaven." She remembered the trip out here, when the trail felt littered with bones, and she'd been sure they travelled the road to the underworld. "I don't know what to say, Theo…"

He leaned in and claimed her mouth. The world tumbled in flashes of light behind her eyelids and the feeling of floating through time and space stole her breath. She placed her injured arm on his shoulder and pressed herself to him as best she could. It didn't feel nearly close enough but there would be time for closeness in their future.

When they broke apart, Theo leaned his forehead against hers. "I'm going to make you the happiest woman in Wylder, Lily."

She touched his lips with hers. "You already have."

A word about the author…

Sarita Leone loves happy endings—in life and on the page.

When she's not busy writing her next novel, this adventure-loving yoga teacher likes to hike, travel, and dance beneath the stars. She studies languages, enjoys making a mess in the kitchen, and never says "no" to fun.

Finding pockets of peace everywhere she goes, this author plans to make every moment of this journey count.

Thank you for purchasing
this publication of The Wild Rose Press, Inc.

For questions or more information
contact us at
info@thewildrosepress.com.

The Wild Rose Press, Inc.
www.thewildrosepress.com